Assignment • • • • •

TREASON

EDWARD S. AARONS

A FAWCETT GOLD MEDAL BOOK

Fawcett Publications, Inc., Greenwich, Conn.

TO RUTH

chapter ONE

DURELL AWOKE knowing that this day was both an end and a beginning. It was not like any other day of his life.

He felt the same, but he was not the same. Overnight, there had been a change. It was nothing tangible as yet; nothing he could see or touch. But the difference was there, hanging heavily in the humid dawn of Washington in August.

He had not slept well. He was not a man given to nerves, since in his profession the nervous ones were those who were most quickly dead. But there had been the quarrel with Deirdre, and that brief telephone talk with General Dickinson McFee.

Staring at the gray dawn light on the ceiling, Durell heard Deirdre's voice again, cool and clear and remote.

"I must go to New York, Sam. Can you come with me?"

"No."

"Will you marry me, Sam?"

"No."

"Not now? Or not ever?"

"Not yet."

He sensed her hesitation, pain and conquered pride. "Is something wrong, Sam?"

"No."

"Is it something with your job?"

"You know better than to ask me that, Dee."

"Please tell me, Sam. I'm hurt. If it's your job, I can understand. I want to understand. And I can wait. I'll wait forever, darling. I love you, Sam."

He said nothing. The telephone hummed.

"Then I guess it's good-by," she whispered.

"Good-by," he said.

So there everything had changed.

Durell got out of bed slowly, aware of the oppressive heat, his sticky skin, his fatigue that struggled against a mounting inner tension. He was a tall man, heavily muscled, with an athlete's grace of movement. His hair was thick and black, and he had a thin, carefully trimmed mustache. His blue eyes were quick and temperamental. He had gambler's hands, inherited from his Grandpa Jonathan, down in the bayou country below New Orleans. His hot Cajun temperament required constant discipline, since a spy who lived by reflex emotions was one who did not live very long. He was a subchief in the K Section of the CIA, and before that he had been with G2 in the Pentagon, and before that with the old OSS in Europe. It was lonely and dangerous work, but he could not imagine now any other kind of existence for himself.

But today that would be changed, too.

The telephone rang in the other room of his small bachelor apartment while he stood under the cold shower. He let it ring. He spooned black Cuban coffee into the pot in his kitchenette and started it perking while he dressed. The telephone rang again. He ignored it and went to the window and looked out at the sunlit street.

The hot morning light made sharp, geometric patterns of black and white on the placid sidewalk. The green sycamore trees stood in patience under the blasting heat. A man in a seersucker suit lounged at the bus stop on the corner, holding a newspaper. Frank Wyatt. An open convertible was parked diagonally across the way from the apartment-house entrance, and a man with a pink bald head fringed with curly yellow hair sat uncomfortably in the sun. Joe Tramm. Durell's mouth tightened and he began a swift, systematic search of his rooms.

He had been out of the apartment all day, which had given them plenty of time to do what had to be done. He found the first bug behind his radio-phonograph, in a corner of the living room. The second bug was tacked to the back of a pigeonhole in his desk. A third was behind a Rivera print over the telephone. He looked at the telephone itself with some suspicion.

Now he knew for certain that it had begun.

He felt anger, and then smiled wryly at himself for resenting the surveillance that he himself had invited.

The telephone rang while he sipped the hot, black Cuban coffee. This time he picked it up.

It was Sidonie Osbourn. Sidonie was the widow of Lew Osbourn, who had been Durell's teammate years ago, in Germany. She was Dickinson McFee's secretary now. She knew nothing about today.

"Sam? Glad I caught you in." She sounded breathless, and an image of her petite French figure drifted across Durell's mind. "I haven't much time, dear. I'm calling from Alexandria. The twins are just off to school. May I be blunt?"

"Go ahead," he said.

"Deirdre spent the night here. What happened between you two yesterday?"

"Nothing."

"I thought you were going to be married next week."

"It's off."

"Oh, Sam!"

"I'm sorry, Sid. I can't explain it now. I can't even talk to you now."

"I've made all the arrangements. I talked to the minister only yesterday morning. Quiet, simple ceremony, just as you and Deirdre wanted it. What is the matter? You sound so strange."

"I feel strange."

"You and Deirdre love each other. I thought you both—"

"She's gone to New York. Forget about it, Sid. Please. I'm sorry for all the trouble you've gone to."

"Aren't you going to call her?"

"No."

"Aren't you going to see her?"

"No."

"Sam, don't be so damned stubborn!"

"Good-by, Sid," he said gently.

He hung up.

He stood still, his blue eyes darkening almost to blackness. The morning heat of Washington invaded the open windows of his apartment, still and breathless and heavy. The corners of his mouth quirked as he looked around the room again. Then he picked up the telephone, hearing the dial tone like a strident insect against his ear.

"Art," he said.

The phone buzzed.

"Art, come on, this is Sam. You're not fooling me."

The buzzing ended with a click. The silence was thick with embarrassment. "Sorry, Sam," came Art Greenwald's voice.

"Why did you bug me?"

"Orders."

"Whose orders?"

"Swayney." Burritt Swayney was chief of the K Section. Durell said simply, "Why check me?"

"It's a hell of a note. I'm just doing what I'm told to do. You know how Security is."

"What am I supposed to have done?"

"I don't know," said Greenwald. "I blew my stack at the Swine Boy when he told me to cover you. He was licking his chops. I said I'd quit first. But you see how it is. You found my bugs?"

"I worked with you too long not to spot them."

"Don't tell Swayney," Art said.

"I won't."

"At least, I didn't put any under your bed, kid."

"Thanks for nothing," Durell said.

He hung up, finished his coffee with two quick swallows, and started the movements of the day that would turn his world upside down.

From under his pillow he took out a thick Manila envelope and slit the seal with his thumbnail. Inside was a sheaf of currency, all in crisp new hundred-dollar bills. He counted the money expertly, his fingers deft and incredibly fast. Twenty thousand. He put the envelope of money inside his gray gabardine coat pocket. From the night table he took his gun, a short-barreled .38 Special, checked the cylinder, dropped a dozen extra cartridges into his side pocket, and fitted the gun inside his coat in the tailored pocket specially designed for it. He took a long look at the apartment before he left. He did not know when, if ever, he would be back.

Treason, Durell thought, was a word with a dirty sound, almost synonymous with spy, a word of darkness and death.

It was not quite eight in the morning, but the tree-lined street was already desolate under the heavy hand of Washington's summer. Durell squinted in the glare of humid sunlight. Frank Wyatt in his seersucker suit still lounged at the bus stop, pretending to study his newspaper. Joe Tramm sat in his convertible nearby, his pink bald head and curly golden fringe of hair in contrast to the wedge of shadow that fell over his narrow face. Durell turned left, and by the time he reached the corner, he heard Tramm's car start and swing in a U turn to follow him.

He knew Tramm and Wyatt thoroughly. Knew their good points as well as their faults. He made it easy for them at first.

Number 20 Annapolis Street was a sedate graystone building with a Georgian façade. A brass plaque beside the front door announced it as the premises of the Johnson-Kimball Company. The front offices off the marble-floored lobby echoed with clattering typewriters from the cover activities that hid the real business conducted here. Number 20 was headquarters for the K Section of the CIA, its rental not listed in the federal budget except as an unidentified sum buried in the General Disbursement funds. The doors that looked like fine walnut paneling were actually of armor-plate steel. The windows were not exactly windows.

There was no visible change in Alex, the guard at the elevator, when Durell entered. Alex was big and blond, with an automatism that perfectly suited his duties. His eyes were always cool and objective as he checked credentials, as if you were a stranger, when in reality he had seen you every day of the week for the past three years.

"Good morning, Mr. Durell. Third?"

"Fourth floor today."

Alex's finger hovered over the button. "Got a pass?"

"Yes." Durell nodded.

"You know the rules, Mr. Durell."

Durell took a card from his wallet and let Alex examine it. He had no right to the card. It did not belong to him. There were only ten in existence, and those ten were delegated to very special members of the Joint Chiefs, the AEC, a member of the White House staff, and two people from the State Department. Durell waited while Alex made up his mind. He could read nothing in the guard's face, and he was inwardly annoyed at the way his pulse quickened like the beat of a tiny hammer inside him.

"Fourth floor," Alex said. "Right."

Durell hoped his relief was not too evident.

He had never been above his own section offices before. A second guard at the elevator exit examined his stolen card with care, lifted shaggy, suspicious brows at Durell, and then jerked his head as if it had been pulled by a puppet's string. The signature could not be ignored.

"Down Corridor C to the Safe Section."

"Thank you," Durell said, and waited.

The shaggy brows lifted again. Cool brown button eyes grew inquisitive. "Waiting for something?"

"The card," Durell said. "May I have it back?"

"We keep it. Check at the White House for it."

"All right. Thanks."

"You have ten minutes to consult the files."

"Thanks again."

He found Corridor C, walking through an armored doorway into the building adjacent to Number 20. Nobody bothered him now. The filing cabinets in the Safe Section reached from floor to ceiling, and a gray-haired anonymous clerk helped him to find what he wanted. The file folder containing the dossiers of three men in Eastern Europe was made readily available to him. Durell noted that his fingers shook very slightly as he took the folder from the clerk's hand, borrowed a Manila envelope in which to stow it, thanked the man, and walked out. It had taken six minutes to steal the dossiers on the most efficient organization maintained by the CIA beyond the Iron Curtain. In his hand he now carried the lives of three brave, brilliant, and desperate men.

When he took the envelope with him down in the elevator, he knew it was done. He had passed the point where any of his acts might be revocable. He was committed. There was no turning back.

He had the feeling that he was being watched as he turned from the elevator on the third floor to his own office. Hazel, his secretary, was on vacation, and Sidonie Osbourn's cousin should have been at his outer desk. Corinne was not there. He strode into his office, paused, looked at his desk, and felt his chest tighten. Someone had carefully examined the papers he had left here last night. Carefully, but not well enough. It was all of a piece with the bugs in his apartment and the watchers out on the street. He dried his hands on a handkerchief, picked up his mail, and tossed it aside without checking any of it.

There were eyes on his back.

Whirling, he saw the girl who stood in the open doorway. Corinne Ybarra had none of Sidonie's petite figure and manner. She was a tall, firm-fleshed girl, disturbing to have in an office where concentrated work had to be done. She did not belong here, and if it hadn't been for Sidonie's pleas, she would not have been employed. But ever since Lew Osbourn was killed, Sidonie had been granted carte blanche in the K Section, working for General McFee. She had argued for Corinne, and Corinne was hired.

The girl looked at ease. She smiled. "Where have you been, Sam?"

He said flatly, "You're in early."

Still smiling, she closed the door and leaned back against it with her hands behind her. She wore a gray skirt that hugged provocative hips, and a creamy sweater with translucent beads. Her dark hair had deep glints of copper in it, like fire seen distantly in the black of night. Her mouth was full and red, suddenly pouting.

"You don't like me, do you?"

"Liking you has nothing to do with anything that goes on in this building. You ought to know that, Corinne."

"What were you doing up in Heaven?"

He stared at her. "Heaven?"

"The Fabulous Fourth Floor. The sanctum sanctorum. The supersecret, inviolate, sacred fourth floor."

"I wasn't there," he said heavily.

She smiled again. "But I saw you, Sam."

"How?"

"I saw the elevator come down. I saw you get off. I was surprised, because poor damned souls such as you and I never get to Heaven. You had an envelope, too—the one in your pocket now. Am I being too curious?"

"Much too curious."

"But it is only because I like you, Sam. Sidonie thinks you are wonderful. Her husband, poor Lew, used to swear by Sam Durell. I am inclined to agree with them. I consider myself lucky to be working for you while Hazel is on vacation." The quiet irony in her throaty voice belied the meaning of her words. She had only a slight accent that gave away her Catalan origin. Her hazel eyes were wide and luminous and intelligent. Opalescent earrings that matched her necklace glinted and shimmered when she shook her head. "I wish you would trust me. I would like to help you, if you would only let me."

He sat down behind the desk. His body felt heavy and

tired, although it was not hot in the office, thanks to the quiet purring of the air-conditioner. He dragged the flat of his hand across his mouth. He wanted a cigarette. "Why should I need help, Corinne?"

"Because you are in trouble, dear," she said.

"What makes you think so?"

"The whole office is talking about it."

"Come here," he said. "Sit down."

She moved with the grace of a jungle animal. He could not resist watching her body. She was aware of this and made no effort to hide her pleasure in it. She sat opposite him at the desk, her back straight, her primness only emphasizing the womanliness of her.

"What are they saying about me, Corinne?" he asked.

"Nothing definite. Just the usual office grapevine. I think people are shocked. You are considered a security risk."

"Who considers me a risk?"

"Mr. Swayney. Dickinson McFee. I don't know." She shrugged delicately. "I don't like to believe it. Sidonie is terribly upset, of course. She's perfectly furious and she is defending you like a little mother cat. But after all, they say—" She paused.

"Go on," Durell urged.

"They say you were once a professional gambler. You have been playing bridge at the Triton Country Club, over in Alexandria. Very regularly. They say you have lost a great deal of money to a certain Colonel Gibney, Henry Gibney, from the Pentagon."

Durell was shaken. So much of it was true, and so much of it was already public knowledge. He told himself that this was to be expected, that it was all planned for and arranged. It was easy to leak rumor, suspicion, threat. But the reality of hearing it from someone else made him feel as if a giant hand had reached inside him and squeezed his organs in a cold and iron grip.

The girl sat there, smiling, waiting for something.

He did not know what she wanted.

"Sam," she said quietly. "Where is Deirdre?"

"In New York today. Why?"

"Sidonie says that your marriage is off."

"Yes. Why?"

She looked at her hands. "I am glad."

"I don't understand why you should be interested."

She stood up, gracefully, smoothly. "You're too much of a man to understand. But I'm glad. Will you meet me for lunch?"

"I'm busy," he said bluntly. "It's not good policy."

"But it is important."

"I don't need help, Corinne," he said, forcing patience. "If you have any dramatic ideas about undercover work, get them out of your head. Most of the work done in this office is routine, clerical analysis and integration of reports from field men abroad. There is no glamour, no danger, no excitement in any of it. It's drudgery. You're in the wrong place here, if you want the other thing. And if you want it, out of some juvenile delusions of adventure, you don't belong out there, either."

"I understand. But *you* wish you were back in the field, don't you?"

"I get restless," he admitted.

"Are you planning to go back to Europe?"

He looked up sharply. "What kind of a question is that?"

She smiled and did not answer. She went to the door and opened it and then turned to face him again. Her wide skirt rustled. "I think it would be wise if you met me for lunch. At Marco's, one o'clock. I dislike waiting. So please be prompt."

She closed the door. It was not an invitation. It was an order.

chapter TWO

HE WENT to see Burritt Swayney. Each step of this day's work was carefully planned and had to be carefully executed.

Swayney, chief of K Section, was a round-bottomed, pear-shaped man with a pursing mouth and cool, codfish eyes. His wife was a thin Bostonian who gave him little satisfaction, and Swayney's one weakness was for women to whom he had no legal attachments. His memory was encyclopedic; his efficiency vied with that of the electronic calculators. He wore a charcoal-gray suit and a tidy blue bow tie and a starched white shirt that remained unwilted despite the August heat.

"Come in, Sam," he said.

Durell closed the office door. "I want to see Dickinson McFee."

"You can't see him."

"Is he in?"

"Not to you."

"All right," Durell said. "Tell me what this is all about."

Swayney lifted wisps of eyebrows. His round face was without guile. "Is something troubling you, Sam?"

Durell's anger was not entirely simulated. "You know damned well. This morning I found some of Art Greenwald's mikes in my apartment. Don't blame him. They were well hidden. Wyatt and Tramm tailed me to work this morning. I couldn't help spotting them, too. What's bothering you, Burritt?"

"Nothing at all," Swayney said blandly. "I happen to be at peace with the world."

Durell leaned both hands on the chief's desk and bent forward. "Am I suspected of something?"

"Routine surveillance, Sam."

"Like hell. You know. You know all about me. Why the check and double check?"

Swayney made steeples of his fat, pink fingers. He looked happy. "Samuel Durell, born 1926, Bayou Peche Rouge, Louisiana, son of Jonathan Durell, Junior, and Mary-Ellen Lamont Durell. Cajun stock. Graduate of Yale, *cum laude*. OSS from 1943 to '45, two years with G-two in Pentagon, service with CIA since March four, 1951. Engaged to marry Deirdre Padgett, of Prince John, Maryland. But marriage plans canceled last night. No bad or vicious habits except a tendency to gamble. Grandfather Jonathan was notorious for it. Still is. Old Mississippi sidewheeler man. You've been playing a lot of bridge at the Triton Country Club. Losing a lot of money, too. Is any of that wrong?"

"You son-of-a-bitch," Durell said softly.

"Don't blame me. You came in here asking for it."

"Does that make me disloyal?"

"We wonder," Swayney said. His jowls were pink. "You'd better get out of here, Sam."

"You lecherous little bastard," Durell said.

"Don't goad me, Sam."

"Then take your tails off me, and stay off my back!"

Swayney said in a rapid singsong, "The primary requisites of an operative of K Section are a cool mind, quick intelligence, an objective viewpoint, and clinical detachment toward problems either personal or involving line of duty."

"To hell with you," Durell said.

"Good day, Sam."

Durell went out. He was shaking with anger.

He tried to see General McFee anyway. Sidonie Osbourn was at her desk in the outer office. Through an open doorway to the left was a room filled with teletype machines and several small Mark III electronic computers. Sidonie was small and delicate, with hair like honey, Gallic eyes slightly uptilted. There were violet smudges under her lashes. She spoke with an accent more pronounced than her cousin Corinne's.

"You can't see McFee," she said, shaking her head.

"Why not?"

"He specifically said he could not see you today if you came asking for him. I'm so sorry, Sam. Will you come to the house for dinner tonight?"

"Thanks. But I doubt if I can make it."

"The children miss you. They will be disappointed."

"Another time," he said. "Sid, can you help me?"

"In any way possible. But if it's about McFee, I'm afraid not. Deirdre spent an unhappy night at my house. She didn't sleep much. Today she's in New York, looking for a new job there. What went wrong, Sam?"

"She'll be grateful for the whole thing," he said roughly. "Just give her a day or two. She won't want to speak to me. I think I'm about to be strung up by the thumbs."

"Don't you think she'll have faith in you?"

"I don't know. It might be too much to ask."

Her distress was genuine. "I heard something— Sam, do you need money to get out of trouble?"

He smiled. "No, Sid. Thanks again. You're a sweetheart. Lew was lucky."

"While he lived, we had something wonderful," she whispered. "Now I have the girls. And what I remember. But don't call me sweetheart, please. Say that to Deirdre, not to me."

"You women," Durell said.

He went down in the elevator to the street. He was acutely

conscious of the envelope that weighted down his pocket, and it seemed to him that everyone he passed must surely know about the material he had stolen from the fourth floor.

The heat pressed down on him like a hand slapped against the nape of his neck. The trees looked lifeless, without motion, gray in the midmorning glare. At the far corner of the street, Joe Tramm drowsed in his open convertible. His bald scalp looked pinker than before. Frank Wyatt was not in sight, but Durell felt his presence without looking too hard for him. He walked to the parking lot where he had left his car, not looking backward or to either side.

The bank on Fourteenth Street was cool and hushed, a marble mausoleum dedicated to finance. The clerk was distantly courteous. Durell opened an account in his own name, depositing the twenty thousand dollars in crisp currency. The clerk was more interested then. He asked Durell's indulgence and went into consultation with a vice-president, who thereafter took personal charge of Durell's new account. There was no question that he would be readily remembered when the time for remembering arrived.

Tramm and Wyatt still dogged him when he paused for lunch. It was time now, Durell decided, to shake them off. And while both men were experts, Durell knew from his own experience that there were limitations to tailing a man. He went into a parking lot as if to reclaim his car, walked through to the exit on the opposite street, and entered a department store by a side doorway. He did not hurry. Mingling with the crowd, he used the escalator to the basement, where government girls shopped on their lunch hour. He bought a pepper mill and a screw-driver, then went up to the stationery counter and bought a Manila folder. Wyatt was still behind him. There was a surge in the crowd toward a side exit where the busses stopped, and Durell let himself be carried by the pressure of human bodies to the second bus in line. He saw Tramm following in the convertible when they pulled out. At the third stop he got off, crossed the street to another shop, then quickened his steps abruptly to leave by the back entrance. A cab stand was nearby. He flagged one, rode to Union Station, changed taxis again, and gave the address of a small hotel out near Rock Creek Park, not five blocks from Annapolis Street.

Nobody was behind him now.

The Park-Crown Hotel was small and residential, the lobby

paneled in dark walnut, cooled by slowly revolving fans in the high ceiling. The clerk nodded when he asked for George Carlton Smith.

"Room Eight-o-two, sir."

Durell rode up in the elevator, walked down the hall with its rows of anonymous shutter doors, and knocked twice on 802.

General Dickinson McFee opened the door for him.

"Come in, Sam. You're right on time."

McFee was a small, gray man with cool, intelligent eyes. His size was forgotten after a man had been a few moments with him; he had the ability to fill any room with the force of his presence. Durell looked around quickly. The room was just a room. Nobody else was in it. Yet it was crowded by ghosts, all pointing fingers of accusation at him. He looked at Dickinson McFee. The General's gray eyes were opaque, telling him nothing.

"Sit down, Sam. You look unhappy. And hot. Not much different from the bayous, I suppose. Drink?"

"Not now."

"I assume you were not shadowed?"

"Tramm and Wyatt are good men," Durell said. "They couldn't help it."

"Yes, they're good. But you're the best I've got."

"I wish you thought otherwise," Durell said. "I wish you had picked anybody else for this rotten job. I don't like it. It's making a mess of everything."

McFee had a small face, an intellectual brow. Eyes like ice, hard and brilliant, devoted. The pressure of his personality grew in the room relentlessly. He stood up and said flatly, "Sam, you knew what to expect when we first talked this over."

"I'm going to lose my girl."

"If she's worth anything at all, you'll get her back."

"My friends look at me as if I have two heads."

"So you do. One for us, one for the other side. Did you get the file?"

Durell took the envelope from his pocket and offered it to the small gray man, but McFee waved it curtly away. "Keep it. We want it found on your person when you're arrested tomorrow for treason and espionage."

"Tomorrow?"

"We've pushed up the target date for your trial. It's a

squeeze. State is in a real flap; so is the White House. I've been called to the Hill twice today, before the Foreign Affairs Committee."

"It's that big?"

"A problem of time has come up. I wish it didn't have to be this way. Don't get careless, Sam. They want me to push you and I told them to go to hell. I don't want to lose you."

Durell waited.

"Be in your apartment tomorrow morning. Make it ten o'clock. You will be arrested there. Swayney will do it. He'll enjoy it. He doesn't like you, Sam."

"All right."

"Which means that Swayney will do a realistic job of it."

Durell waited.

"You will be tried tomorrow, in the afternoon, before a special loyalty board. It's a squeeze, as I said," McFee paused. "Did you deposit the money?"

"Yes."

"No other problems?"

Durell thought of Corinne Ybarra.

"Something, Sam?"

"No," Durell said.

It was hot in the little hotel room. The windows were all open, but a furnace blasted outside in the green of Rock Creek Park. When the air stirred occasionally through the wooden shutter door, it had a brassy smell that only emphasized the suffocating heat. Durell sweated. His shirt stuck to his back.

"You can still get out," McFee said suddenly. "If you dislike it this much."

"I don't like it. Who would? But I'll do it. Do you tell me now what it's all about?"

McFee nodded. His gray hair was smooth and thick, cropped short. His small face was hard. Like stone. Like his voice. "This is the last time we may discuss it until you find the traitor in K Section, Sam. You don't communicate with me in any way after you walk out of this room. We will be strangers. I shall despise you. I'll throw every charge in the book at you. It will look good. It has to look good, in order to be convincing. Otherwise, you're dead. When you get what I want, and not before then, you can talk to me again. Is that clear?"

"Yes. But I wish you'd take this file off my hands."

"You have to be arrested with it in your possession."

"It's risky."

"It's a calculated risk. Hell, I've told you, those people have to be convinced that you've gone sour. They won't be fooled by anything else."

"And after the trial tomorrow?"

"Your escape is arranged. Get as rough about it as you please. Just don't kill anybody. Then you're on your own."

"Like a fox in the bayou with Lem Hardway's hounds after it," Durell said. His smile was thin. He still sweated. "The twenty thousand you had me deposit in my name is just window-dressing?"

"To show you've been accepting money. From somewhere. Don't say where. Don't offer any guesses. You're a clam."

"And my losses to Gibney at the Triton Club?"

"You needed the money, you were desperate, so you broke your own private rules about gambling. Sorry, Sam. It was for your Grandpa Jonathan down in Bayou Peche Rouge. He's desperately ill."

Durell was startled. "Does he know?"

"Nothing. He'd kill you, wouldn't he?"

"He's a proud old man."

"He'll be prouder, later on. If it works. If you live."

"And Colonel Gibney? It wasn't easy to keep losing to him. He's not a very good card player," Durell said.

"He hasn't been good in any direction since his son disappeared in East Berlin," McFee snapped.

"Is he our man?"

"We don't know. We think so. We think he worked with someone in K Section to lift the dossiers on the Triangle Group." McFee got up and walked to the window and looked through the thin curtain at the dusty green of the park. From the street came the sudden sound of a taxi horn, the shrill yelp of a child, a woman's scolding voice. A radio began to play in one of the rooms down the corridor. The music was loud and rhythmic. McFee drew a deep breath. "We have three men working for us on the other side of the Curtain. One of them is a Russian, Igor Kobyschev, a minor MGB clerk at Number Two Dzersinski Square. His son was killed by the Nazis in the Pripet Marshes in 1942. His brother lives in a small town in upstate New York. A farmer. Igor sends material to Herman Warsciusko, a Pole who lives in Gdynia. Warsciusko is—or was—the director of a small shipping and maritime department in the Scandinavian trade. The third leg of the triangle is a man simply named Antonio. Mixture of Rumanian and Italian. Handsome devil. Likes the ladies. Oddly enough, he's in Hungary. Budapest. We've got a great amount of valuable information from them. They can never be replaced. But they're going to die. All three of them."

"Why?" Durell asked.

"Somebody stole part of their dossiers from the Safe Section at Number Twenty Annapolis." McFee made a chopping gesture. "You have the rest of the dope on them in your pocket. The rest of what they need. The stolen part has their names in code. The file you took fits the file that was stolen. If they get yours, some throats will be cut."

"I see."

"So be careful."

"When was the first theft?"

"Last Thursday. It wasn't the first, though."

"Have you heard from any of those three men since?"

"No."

"Do you think the information on them is already out of the country?"

"Not yet. We've checked. But it can't be bottled up. A code letter to any of the Western NATO countries, an agent in Paris, Copenhagen, Athens—you name it—and it's relayed to Moscow. All three will die. They may or may not talk. It's arranged and understood that they try to die. But you can't tell. Lately, just when things start to look easier on the international scene, we've had leaks like this that threaten to blow the roof off. Peace is a delicate blossom, Sam, always threatened by blights. The trouble with these thefts is that each one is ultrasensitive. Usually, when they get one of our men or break up an apparatus we've built, they keep quiet about it. Just to keep us worried and wondering. But not lately. Lately, each one has been publicized. It's like a series of dynamite caps going off near an ammo dump. Hell to pay if it keeps up. You have to stop it. Find out who's leaking information from K Section. Stop the transmission of their names to the MGB. Not an easy job."

Durell sensed something more. He waited. McFee walked up and down, then took a folded sheet of typescript from his pocket. Attached to it was a newspaper clipping. "Look at this."

The clipping was from a Communist daily in Budapest, *Népszava*. It was dated 22 June. The typewritten sheet was a translation from the Hungarian:

"The following volunteers for resettlement in the Pavlodar region of Kazakhstan may sell for cash or on commission their surplus furniture and household goods, on appraisement at your home. Leave address at the Commission Warehouse, Bizományi Aruház VIII, Kinizai utca 4, Telephone 621-223."

Under this notice was a list of perhaps one hundred names. Durell replaced the clipping in the envelope and returned it to Dickinson McFee. His face was impassive.

McFee said, "All that is a small facet of the Communist program of deportation and population transfer to break up silent resistance. They move indigenous ethnic groups from Hungary, Rumania, the Carpathian Ukraine, and the Baltic states to Asia, Tatar country, and transfer Tatar and Kirghiz peoples into Europe. The Soviets are transforming Europe's ethnography daily. It's nothing to do with us— except for one item."

Durell watched the small general quietly.

"One of these so-called volunteer deportees," McFee said in a heavy tone, "is Antonio's girl."

Durell blew out air.

"Antonio has been out of contact with the others in the Triangle since this happened. He's insane over that girl. He's made assassination threats, should anything happen to her. Now it's happening."

"All this has been checked?"

"And double-checked. He's hunting with a gun. You know who for. If he kills anybody in their upper governmental echelons, and if this leak gets his name to Dzersinski Square as one of our agents, there will be hell to pay. They'll scream we're on a program of assassination. The man he's after is not too balanced, emotionally. Any personal threat could bring down this house of cards we call peace."

"Can we stop Antonio?"

"No. We can only pray. And keep them from knowing anything more about him than the code name that was stolen."

"It may already be too late," Durell pointed out.

"Yes. That's why we're squeezing this."

"And you think Colonel Gibney is mixed up in it?"

"I accuse nobody. Not yet. But Gibney has been fishing for information on the Triangle from some of our people. It was reported to me. That's why you've been playing cards with him." McFee smiled tiredly. "I know it was a bad thing for you, Sam."

"I like to gamble. Not to lose."

"Gibney will offer a settlement with you. He lives high off the hog. He needs money. We think his son, Roger, is being held by our opponents in this rotten game, and we think Roger is being used as a lever to make Gibney do a little work for the other side. Not a nice thing. None of it is nice, eh?"

"Go on," Durell said.

"Nothing much more. You owe Gibney a lot of money now. You get mud in your eye tomorrow. You lose friends and alienate people. You're accused of treason—and you escape. You contact Gibney for help. We'll see if they take you into their club."

"Suppose he turns down the bait?"

"Then we're wrong."

"Whom do you suspect in K Section?"

"Nobody. Everybody. We're up against a problem of time, Sam. We may not be able to help our three men. But maybe others can be saved. That's why I'm pushing you. It won't be easy. Still want to do it?"

"It's my job," Durell said.

McFee looked at him for a hard moment. Durell could not begin to guess what the small man was thinking. A pigeon landed on the stone window ledge and cooed and burbled and rustled its feathers. It looked dusty and tired. Durell suddenly saw before him a succession of gray, tired days, of long hours of disgrace, accusation, despair, and danger.

"You understand," McFee said quietly, "nobody is to know what you're doing. Other men have had similar jobs, in other times. It wasn't easy for them. Or for their families. Or for the folks who liked them and loved them. You don't confide in anyone, naturally."

"I know."

"Is Deirdre in New York today?"

"Yes."

"You broke with her deliberately?"

"Yes."

"She is not to suspect anything except what appears on the surface. Or Sidonie Osbourn."

"They don't suspect. They're just worried about me."

McFee stood up. "That's it, then. You're the man."

"Set a thief to catch a thief?"

McFee smiled. "Or a spy to catch a spy."

"Yes."

"You'll be alone, Sam. Be careful. If they take you into the club, be doubly careful. But make it convincing."

"I will."

"You start with Gibney. We're pretty sure of him. He's sour. But he's not the one we want. The one we're ultimately after is someone right here in K Section. Somebody you've worked with, somebody you drink with. Maybe somebody you've made love to and slept with. Whoever it is, it's the last person you might suspect. It might even be me," McFee said. "That's the way you're to look at it."

"All right," Durell said. "Even you."

The interview was over. Durell felt oddly reluctant to leave. He knew it would be the last friendly conversation he could have with anyone for a long time.

"Good luck," McFee said.

They shook hands.

chapter THREE

THE TRITON CLUB was a remodeled Virginia colonial of old rose brick, with lawns that swept down to the banks of the Potomac. It was a supper club, eminently respectable, frequented by brass from the Pentagon and upper-echelon people from State and Defense who desired a cool, quiet evening. There was a colonnaded veranda that rivaled Lee's residence, old live oaks that formed an avenue of the driveway, and a refreshing river breeze. White sails bent and bellied on the blue surface of the water as Durell drove up the shell driveway.

Colonel Henry Gibney was not there. He had a drink at

the bar, a frosted julep served by a competent waiter in a starched mess jacket; he sat on the veranda and looked at the boats on the river; he chatted with an Air Force major who seemed to know him.

He thought of Deirdre.

He thought of Bayou Peche Rouge, of his boyhood in the Delta swamps, the long, long days of heat and dust, and his home aboard the old Mississippi side-wheeler fast in the mudflats, the gambling shop that Grandpa Jonathan had made into a home. It was long ago, and all of it belonged to another, far distant world. A clean and simple world of schooling, hunting, fishing, of exploring the Indian mounds and creepy, shadowed *chenières*. The world was uglier now, too complex, filled with forces that pushed and pulled at a man, twisting him in all directions until his head spun dizzily and he became easy prey for the shouted command, the glib slogan, the hammered reiteration of crass propaganda.

He thought of tomorrow: the trial, the disgrace, the loneliness ahead.

Well, what did you expect, an egg in your beer? You're a spy, you do what you're told to do. You're told to give up your girl; so you hurt her, you drive her away. You're told to give up your honor and your friends. And maybe to give up life itself. And you do it all.

But you don't have to like it.

Durell was not a conscious patriot. But when he looked across the Potomac, at the gently swelling hills under the hot sun, the peaceful houses, this river and this land were a part of him that he loved fiercely, above all else. He never spoke of this. It was part of him like the air he breathed, woven into the texture of his blood and flesh and bones. Yet his devotion to his work did not confine him to this place or that or to any particular people in the world. If someone had called him a humanitarian, he would have laughed. . . .

Usually Gibney was here by two o'clock, every afternoon. He was not here today. Of all days. He told himself not to worry, but he could not help worrying.

Long ago, and until recently, he had traveled a lonely way, knowing that death waited with a hungry appetite for anyone in his profession whose attention was distracted by the love and affection of others. Deirdre had changed all that.

He was in love with her. He wanted her. He could feel a twist of desire in him when her image, cool and lovely, drifted across his mind. Perhaps she would stand by him, trying to understand. But there were limits to the strain one could place upon human relations. He had been cruel to her; he had built a protective wall between them. It had to be done. Yet there was in him an overwhelming desire to go to her and tell her what he was doing, and this desire alarmed him, because he had never known this conflict before.

He returned to the bar and had another drink. Gibney had not shown up. He had promised to be here promptly at two. It was very late now. Gibney had insisted on the appointment, for a settlement of the seven thousand dollars Durell had managed to lose to him.

The wind died on the river, and the heat settled over the clubhouse like a slowly lowered blanket. The glare of the sun made Durell squint when he looked out through the windows of the bar. He saw Colonel Gibney walking across the oyster-shell driveway toward the bar entrance, with a girl in a thin summer frock clinging to his fat arm. The girl was Corinne Ybarra.

Durell finished his drink and went to meet them.

Gibney was a portly man, over six feet tall, with white hair the color of week-old snow. His face was brick-red from the sun, and his pale eyes were bloodshot. He had a loud, hearty manner as false as his booming laugh, and Durell did not like him. It had been quite an effort to force himself to lose at cards to this man.

"Sam Durell!" Gibney shouted. "Sorry we're late. I was showing Corinne our little place at Cramden Beach. You know Cramden?"

"I've heard of it."

"Guess you thought you'd lost me, hey?"

"I didn't think I'd have the luck."

Gibney laughed again. He always laughed. It didn't mean anything. Durell looked at Corinne. She was smiling, but there was a great deal of meaning in her hazel eyes, in the curve of her rich and promising lips. Her bare shoulders were creamily tanned above the gray of her cotton frock. The hot sunlight sparked brush fires in her dark hair.

"You disappointed me for lunch, Sam. I waited," she said softly.

"Sorry."

"You're not sorry at all. But I forgive you. I feel as if I shall always be forgiving you. Do let us have a drink, shall we? I am parched."

They returned to the bar. Gibney ordered, his manner expansive. But there was a guarded look about him as he surveyed the quiet room, with its colonial prints and brick fireplaces. The Triton was not crowded yet, although in half an hour, when the floodgates opened at the government offices up the river, there would be a deluge of voices, clinking china and glassware, and music. For the moment, Durell was grateful for their relative privacy.

"You wanted to see me, Henry," he said.

"Yes, yes. But that can wait."

"You made it sound urgent."

"Did I? Well, your credit is good." Gibney laughed again. His face was very red, his eyes swimming in yellow-red liquid. He smoothed his thick white hair. He had square military shoulders under his Palm Beach suit, but his paunch had got out of control and destroyed the briskly efficient look he hoped to achieve. "There's no hurry now, Sam."

"I got what you asked me for," Durell said quietly.

"Eh?" Gibney was startled. He licked his lips. "Look here, I wasn't really serious."

"I was. Let's go where we can talk," Durell said.

Corinne frowned with mild annoyance. "What kind of secrets do you boys have that I can't hear?"

"It's a personal matter," Durell said. "Please excuse us."

"I will, but I don't like it."

Durell put a hand under Gibney's elbow and urged the fat man up from his bar stool. He sensed a reluctance in the other, and for a moment Gibney silently resisted him. Then the Colonel bolted the rest of his drink, muttered an apology to Corinne, and walked with Durell to the veranda. Durell led the way down the shell walk to the riverbank No one was nearby. The boats had cleared off the broad surface of the water. The sun slashed at them. There was no wind at all.

"How long have you known Corinne?" Durell asked suddenly.

"Eh? Oh, she's a fine girl. She visits at Cramden Beach quite a bit. Lovely child. Lovely." Gibney hesitated. "Never seen you at Cramden, Sam. Lots of fun there."

"I hear it's rather decadent."

"Nonsense. Private colony for exhausted government people, that's all. Chance to recoup our vitality, that sort of thing, without a mob around. The world is a crowded place these days, my boy. Privacy around Washington is at a premium. Why not come down to my shack tonight rather than talk here? It might be better."

"Suddenly, you seem afraid to be seen with me," Durell said.

"It isn't that. Not a bit of it. I just heard—you were in trouble, that's all."

"Did you hear that from Corinne?"

"Well, some of it. But there's other talk." Gibney licked his full lips. His eyes were like cloudy milk in the glare of the sun. "Look, about that seven thousand you owe me—"

"I'm ready to pay off."

"In cash?"

"No."

"Frankly, I could use the money," Gibney said. "Cramden is expensive. You lost it to me fair and square, you know. Gentleman's debt."

"Not in money," Durell said flatly.

Gibney's mouth stretched briefly in a quick, meaningless smile. "You didn't take me seriously about that other thing, did you?"

"Yes."

"Good Lord, man, I didn't mean—"

"You meant it," Durell said.

"But I was—I had too much to drink. I didn't realize you would—"

"You're being blackmailed by the Reds for your son's safety. They've got him over there and they'll kill him unless you do something for them. You told me all about it."

"Yes, but—"

"I'm ready to help you, and pay off what I owe you."

"You must be mad! I was drinking too much, I didn't know what I—" Gibney paused, his voice suddenly breaking. He looked down at the dusty grass underfoot. They were almost at the river's edge. "I want to help my son," he whispered. "I'm at my wits' end. They'll kill him. They'll torture him. I'm sorry I told you about it. I was desperate that night. They had just sent me photographs of him."

"Who contacted you?" Durell asked.

"I can't tell you that."

"What's their price?"

"Information. From K Section."

"Then I have it for you," Durell said.

Gibney looked at him. For a moment there was a spark of keen intellect, deep suspicion, and anger behind his fat, flushed features. Then it all collapsed into soft, red jelly. He looked as if he were going to cry. He turned from Durell and took a few quick steps back toward the clubhouse, then halted. His shoulders sagged.

"I heard that you are under suspicion, Durell," he said hoarsely. "I don't want to get caught. I want to help Roger, but I don't want to ruin everything by getting caught at it. It would be as if I'd killed him myself, if he ever heard about it."

"But you got information from them before, from K Section, didn't you?" Durell asked sharply.

"What makes you say that?"

"I'm not the first person you contacted over there. It didn't begin with me. You got your hooks into me for seven grand, and I'm willing to pay off to help you out. And to get you to tear up the chits. Why didn't you work on your first contact, instead of me?"

Gibney looked broken. "I don't know what you're talking about."

"Do you want the stuff, or don't you?" Durell demanded.

"I—I don't know what to do. I didn't realize you—"

"Are you afraid?"

"Yes," Gibney whispered. His eyes looked sick. "And I'm damned to the depths of my soul."

Durell pretended anger. "Look, I took some big chances getting that file of information for you. It may kill several good people. I'm not sentimental, and I don't ever wave the flag. I told you before, when we first met, that I regard this as a dog-eat-dog world. It's the Big Me first, last, and always, and to hell with the suckers who aren't quick enough or smart enough to stay on their feet. I risked everything to get clear of your hooks, and now you're putting on this big deal of an act, pretending your conscience bothers you."

"It does," Gibney whispered. "I'm sick with it."

"Do you want them to torture and cripple your only son? Do you want them to kill him, or maybe worse, turn him into a blind and brainless idiot?"

"No. No. I want to help him."

"I have the papers with me," Durell said briskly. "Do you want them now?"

Gibney swallowed loudly. "Not here."

"Make a date, then."

Gibney drew a shaken breath. His face was tormented, hating Durell, hating the world around him. He stared at the river, at the clubhouse, and at the huge red ball of the setting sun that seemed to finger the sky with hands of fire.

"Damn you. Come over to my place at Cramden Beach tonight," he said. "Bring the—documents with you."

"What time?"

"Make it late. I have some guests coming for a barbecue and a swim. Make it after midnight."

"All right," Durell said.

"I'm sorry about all this," Gibney said. "I don't know where it will end. They've promised to release Roger if I do this last thing for them. Do you think they'll keep their word?"

"If it suits them," Durell said.

Gibney hesitated. "You really got what you said you could get for me?"

Durell tapped his breast pocket. "All here."

"God help me. And them." Gibney drew a deep breath. "Tonight, then. Cramden Beach. Can you find my place, or shall I—"

"I'll find it," Durell said. "Let's get back to Corinne. She's a restless woman."

The bar was crowded when they returned, and two Air Force colonels were drinking with Corinne. She seemed happy enough, oblivious of their long absence, although her eyes did not miss Durell's tall figure as he came in from the veranda with Gibney. A small orchestra was playing in the dining room. Gibney became his loud, hearty self the moment he reached the bar, as if he could turn his personalities on and off with the flick of a switch. He drank quickly and greedily, then suggested dinner. It was growing dark outside when Durell at last made his excuses and rose from the table to leave.

"Take me home, Sam," Corinne said, rising also. "I want to talk to you."

Gibney protested. "Honey, you said you were coming to the beach tonight."

"Later, darling. I want to chat with Sam first. I'll find my way there, never fear."

Durell did not argue about it. An attendant brought his car from the lot. Corinne's perfume was light and delicate as she sat close to him on the front seat. She was silent until they were on the highway to the Potomac bridges, and then she said quickly, "Take the next left, Sam. Please drive slowly. I have a lot to say to you."

"You're building up something in your mind that just isn't there," Durell told her. "You're being melodramatic without reason."

"Perhaps I just like to be with you."

"I thought you were interested in Colonel Gibney."

"I am. For other things."

"Such as?"

"Allow me my feminine secrets. Turn left here, please."

He did as she suggested. The road was a small, winding lane between tall oaks and sycamores, and there was a coolness under the interlaced branches of the trees, as if they had entered a long underground tunnel. The sun had set, and dusk crept over the Virginia countryside. There was no other traffic on the blacktop road.

"Where are we heading?" he asked.

"Nowhere. Everywhere. Heaven," she said. "Or hell."

"You seem to prefer to talk in riddles."

"That depends on how obtuse you choose to be. Be nice to me, Sam. I really don't know how to be subtle. I just know that from the moment we met at Sidonie's house, I've wanted to be near you, that's all."

He thought of Deirdre. "You know I'm in love with someone else."

"Are you? You said you wouldn't marry her."

"That may change," he said.

"You don't truly love her. You only think you do. You look lonely; perhaps you are lonely. And Deirdre won't stand by you when you need—friends."

"And what does that mean?"

"It means that I know you're in trouble and that you're doing something desperate and terribly wrong in order to get out of it. I want to help you."

"Why?"

"I told you, dear. I just want to."

The breeze stirred by the car's passage moved her dark

hair. It had lost its brush-fire lights with the coming of dusk, and now looked jet black, thick and lustrous. She was a beautiful, desirable girl. And although Durell knew women as well as any man could know them, he did not understand this woman at all. She was making it plain that she loved him and wanted him; she made no real secret of offering herself to him, if he would only say the word. Yet something about her did not ring true to his trained senses. He wished he knew more about her background.

He felt her warm thigh against his as he drove, then her hands touched him lightly, and without warning she delved into his pocket and plucked out the file he had taken from the Safe Section. He made an involuntary gesture and the car swerved crazily, rode up an embankment, smashed through low-hanging branches, and bounced hard on the road again. Anger surged in him.

"Give me that," he snapped. He reached for the envelope as she drew back, smiling. "Corinne! Hand it over."

She laughed throatily. "Watch the road, darling. You'll kill us both."

He braked to an abrupt, screaming stop, and dust swirled up in a thick, silent cloud over the car. The motor ticked. In the evening twilight he heard the sound of a brook, the sleepy twitter of a bird. There was woodland on both sides of the road, pressing in close, and not a house or a light in sight.

"What do you think you're doing?" he asked the girl.

"This is what you took from the fourth floor, isn't it?"

"Don't be a fool."

She held the envelope with exaggerated delicacy between her fingertips. Her eyebrows arched. "I knew you had taken something, Sam. I felt the paper in your pocket. Perhaps you'd like to wrestle for it?"

"Corinne—"

Lights flickered in the rear mirror.

Durell looked back, and the lights vanished. In the gray twilight he saw the movement of another car easing up the lonely lane behind him. Alarm jangled in him.

Corinne laughed softly.

He twisted away from her, thumbed the starter, kicked the motor to life. Corinne still held the envelope. He ignored it. His car jounced back onto the road and he tramped hard on the gas. Behind them, the headlights flickered up again, came on with a rush while he still gathered speed.

There came a sudden snapping sound, and a star appeared in the windshield, centered by a small bullet hole. The gunshot sounded an instant later, as an afterthought.

"What—" Corinne said.

Durell swung the car in a tight, sharp curve of the road. The way lifted up to the top of a long, rolling rise. The wind of their passage made a sullen roaring noise.

"Who are they?" Durell gritted.

"I—I don't know. Was that a shot? I don't—"

"Don't lie, you bitch. You got me out here. You knew they would come. Who hired you to do it?"

Her voice lifted high, unnatural in pitch. "Honestly, Sam, I didn't! Believe me!"

He risked a sidelong glance at her. Corinne's face was pale and taut in the twilight. He snapped on his headlights to puncture the gloom ahead. The car lifted over the crest of the wooded hill, swooped down a curving descent, and rumbled wildly over a small wooden bridge. There was only desolate brush and woodland on every side. Behind them, the other car was gaining inexorably, closing the gap between them.

There was another shot. And another.

Both missed.

Corinne made a small, queer sound in her throat.

Anger and chagrin rode with Durell as he urged the car to its limits. The road grew narrower and changed abruptly from blacktop to gravel. The car behind drew closer. The headlights winked and bounced and glared, and lances of brightness slashed Durell's eyes. The road twisted left, right, left again. The gravel changed to dirt. Pebbles hammered and rattled under the tires. The wheels caught in deep ruts and they swerved wildly. Corinne screamed. It was totally dark now. They plunged ahead as if boring through a black, twisting tunnel.

The pursuing car was only fifty feet behind them.

Something white flickered in the road ahead. A wooden, painted barrier. Red reflector buttons winked and shimmered.

Durell cursed and slammed on the brakes.

The car slued, left the road to slash through underbrush. Durell felt himself lifted as they rose on two wheels, then slammed down again with a bone-jarring crash. The barrier rushed at them with perilous speed. His headlights lanced beyond the white boards and topped trees that leaned into a deep ravine beyond where the road ended. Dust roiled up around them and then the car stopped, rocking, only a few feet from the fence.

The other car slowed to a halt behind them.

"Get out," Durell said to the girl.

"But you can't—"

He leaned over and snapped open the door and shoved her hard. She fell from the car. He vaulted to the ground after her, glimpsing the Manila envelope she still clutched in her hand. Her face was twisted by terror as she looked back; her dark hair was in loose strands across her cheek. Three dim shapes came running toward them.

There was no moon, no stars. Durell reached into his car and snapped off the headlights. Darkness, except for the twin glaring beams from the other car, folded around them. He grabbed for Corinne's free hand.

"Give me the file," he said harshly. "Quick!"

"They have guns," she whispered.

He pulled the envelope from her fingers, thrust it into his pocket, took her hand again, and ran toward the barrier. They were pursued by a hoarse shout of command. A gun cracked. Past the barrier, the brush made a thick tangle of growth, and the sides of the ravine pitched sharply down into deeper blackness. Durell felt a burning sensation in his throat. The girl stumbled, dragged him backward as he started to slide down the embankment. Water chuckled darkly far below.

"Sam, please. I can't—" she wailed.

"Shut up," he said.

From above, three dim shapes suddenly made gray outlines against the faintly luminous sky.

"Durell!"

They knew his name. They knew what he had for them.

The girl tripped and fell again. He thought of abandoning her, but there was an anger in him that was reflected in the iron grip he kept on her wrist. They had been waiting for him to leave the Triton Club. They knew all about him. She led him down this dark way deliberately, knowing about the others. His hatred was like black acid inside him.

The sound of running water was nearer now. He scrambled down the slope, slammed into the invisible trunk of a tree, and lost his hold on the girl. She gave a little cry and lurched away. Branches crashed and crackled behind and above him. There were no more shouts. The chase was carried on in grim silence.

He went on. The girl was nearby, but beyond his reach now. The darkness in the brush was a blindfold over his eyes. He paused, sucked in a great breath, and pulled his gun from his pocket. There was no sense in further flight. Already one of the men was beyond him, circling wide, obviously familiar with the terrain. His dim shadow flickered for a moment against the gleam of the creek far below. Durell got his back against the wide, slanting trunk of an old birch. A branch snapped nearby and he lifted the gun, finger taut on the trigger. Corinne stumbled out of the shadows and fell against him.

"Sam, please," she whispered. Her mouth was against his cheek as she leaned on him. Her dress was torn, and her body gleamed softly through the ripped gray cotton. Her skin was moist. "I didn't do this to you. Believe me, I didn't!"

"Durell!"

It was a voice like iron, harsh, commanding. It seemed to come from everywhere in the dark underbrush surrounding them.

He did not answer.

"Durell, give it up! Let the girl go!"

The gun felt wet in his hand.

The creek chuckled and giggled at him.

Corinne pressed hard against him. "Sam . . ."

He pushed her away. She gave a little cry and fell, losing her balance on the precarious slope. There came a sudden rush of movement from two sides of the tree that sheltered him, and he triggered the gun twice, hearing the shots slam in echoes back and forth from the sides of the wild ravine. Then they were on him like a dark wave, a deluge of silent, ferocious strength. His gun was torn away. Something struck his head and he went down on hands and knees, swinging wildly in cold rage. He seemed to keep falling endlessly, down and down, and as he fell he heard the girl's scream rise against the black night that enveloped him.

chapter FOUR

SOMEONE SHOOK HIM, called his name.

The voice came from a great distance above him, and the hands on him seemed to be shaking someone else, as if he were detached from his own body, yet an objective part of himself. Water trickled coldly, and he was aware of a sharp, wet chill. Voices muttered for a time. He pushed away at the hands on him, annoyance strong in him.

"Durell, can you hear me?"

There was a cunning in him, and he did not move or reply. Something sharp pressed painfully against his cheek. Water moved coldly over one foot. He opened his eyes a bit. Nothing. Darkness. But shadows moved in the dark. The pain in his cheek was an intolerable burning sensation, and he moved his head away from it. A stone, a sharp pebble. That was better now.

"Durell!"

Men towered over him, spread-legged, seen in distortion from where he sprawled on the pebbly bank of the creek. The trees slid and swooped and wavered high above, then steadied into perspective. Stars shone like polished chrome against a velvet night sky. His throat ached. There was a pain in his ribs. His left hand clutched fingersful of pins and needles.

"He's awake," someone said.

"He's all right. Hardheaded Cajun. Son-of-a-bitch."

"Take it easy, Amos."

"Who was he playing games with?"

"He'll tell us. Sam Durell is all right."

"The son-of-a-bitch."

Durell tried to sit up. There were two men, not three, and they stepped back a little, watching him with grave, anonymous faces shadowed by the trees and the starlight. He saw he was at the very bottom of the ravine, where the creek flowed over smooth dark rocks. High up on the slope was the white-painted barrier where the road ended. There

had been a bridge up there once. He must have rolled and
fallen all the way down the rugged, brushy slope. And his
clothing was ripped and torn, one pocket hanging in a loose,
open flap by a fragile thread. He felt for his gun. It was
gone. He felt for the envelope file. It was gone.

He began to retch suddenly, sickness rushing up in him
like an acid tide.

The two men did not touch him or help him. They stood
and watched in silence.

The waters of the creek chuckled, and early katydids sang
a ululating paean to the August night. His sickness came in
waves, and gradually subsided, leaving him weak and shaken.
He sat back, leaning on his hands, and looked up at the two
men.

"Who are you?" he asked.

The taller man had a long, aquiline nose and the thinly
shadowed, bony face of a classic conspirator. He showed his
dislike of Durell clearly. "I'm Hackett," he said. "This is
Jones. We got a John Doe call you were out here, in trouble."

"I don't know any Hackett or Jones," Durell said.

"I'm with the Q Committee."

Durell looked at the smaller man. "You?"

"M.I., Pentagon."

"Do you have to carry Hackett on your back?"

Jones shrugged. "Hackett got the tip. He works for himself. Not out of our budget. It's his privilege."

"McFee sent you?"

Hackett replied thickly, "We don't work for McFee. The
Q Committee has no strings on it. You're under arrest, you
treasonous bastard."

Durell stood up. He made it slowly, with deliberate care.
His legs trembled for a moment, then steadied. When he
was sure he wouldn't fall down, he swung as hard as
he could at Hackett. It was like hitting a stone wall with a
fly-swatter. There was little strength in his arms, and the
momentum of his swing made him stumble and pitch forward. Hackett laughed, a choked and eager sound. The short-
er man, Jones, caught Durell and steadied him and pulled
him away from his partner.

"Leave him alone, Amos."

Hackett's voice shook with anger. "Don't get in my way,
Jonesy. I warn you. He's my baby. I'll handle him. You can

see how he is, huh? Hotheaded Cajun bastard. A lousy rat. He doesn't have it with him."

Durell said, "You look familiar, Hackett."

"You'll wish you were never born to see me," Hackett spat.

"You were here before. With somebody else. Not Jones. It was two other guys. In the dark."

"You got stones in your head."

"I remember you," Durell said.

"You'll pray to forget me, Cajun."

Durell looked at Jones. Jones was a short man in his middle thirties, compact, bull-shouldered, with straw hair and a round face. His eyes were calm, intelligent, a little worried. He didn't believe what Durell said. His mouth was grave.

Durell said, "Who tipped you I was here?"

"Hackett told it. John Doe."

"Not Jane?"

"What makes you think it might have been a woman?"

"I was brought here by a woman," Durell said. "Ask Hackett. He followed me from the Triton Club and helped to mug me. Ask him. Look at him. What kind of game is he playing?"

Hackett's thin, dark face was ugly, carved in angles and planes by the newly flooding moonlight. His voice rasped. "Don't throw dust around, Durell. What did you do with the file you swiped from K Section?"

"You've got it," Durell said flatly. "You slugged me and took it, less than an hour ago. So to hell with you."

"You feel that tough?" Hackett asked.

"I'm feeling better all the time."

Jones said, "Easy, Amos. Who was the woman, Durell?"

"Ask Hackett. He followed her when she led me down this garden path. He's lying. He has the file. He knows all the answers."

"I've had enough," Hackett said.

Jones spoke again. "Take it easy. Well, Durell?"

Durell said nothing. The retching sickness still quivered inside him. He thought of Corinne Ybarra. She had led him here. She had lured him to this lonely cul-de-sac where he had been mugged and robbed of the files McFee expected to retrieve tomorrow. Despair settled around him like a dark mantle. He did not know what to do or say. He looked at Hackett and he was not really sure that Hackett was one of the three men who had followed him. It had been dark. It had happened too quickly. Yet there was a feeling in him that his shot at the Q man had hit a hidden mark. It didn't make sense. If Hackett was one of the muggers, he had the file. Or did he? Not to judge by the way he acted, held in check only by Jones's official status. Hackett had no real standing in the government. Was Hackett here because he had to be here or else tip his hand?

Durell had heard of the staff of the Q Committee, that extragovernmental, private organization headed by former Senator Hereward Quenton, of Texas. Bantam rooster in a ten-gallon hat, foaming at the mouth at subversives, loyalty risks, Reds, foreigners, damyankee liberals, Harvard eggheads. Comical, but not too comical, with uncounted millions behind him. He loaned private investigators to various Congressional committees, serving without pay to the government, but on Quenton's private payroll. The Q men were an embarrassment that had to be accepted or political axes would start to swing. Where had Quenton gained such influence? Politics, millions, a screaming, ranting press that made honest government employees wriggle and squirm and knuckle under rather than fight the avalanche of pressure Quenton could bring to bear on you.

All right, Durell thought, you're only guessing about Hackett. Forget him. You expected to face tomorrow with a clear inner conscience, with no real damage done by McFee's plan. The file you took would be safely back where it belonged. But now it was gone. And the roof had caved in.

"All right, let's go," Jones said finally.

Hackett pushed him roughly toward the slope that lifted up to the dead end of the road.

"Durell, I'd like to talk to you here, but Jones is too goddamn soft to work you over the way you ought to be worked on."

"We don't do things that way," Jones said quietly.

"Which is too bad. He'd goddamn well talk to me, or he'd be floating down the creek on his belly." Hackett paused, lifted his narrow head with a twitch. "Jonesy, he's already got a few lumps. Nobody could say who gave him what, if we swiped him a couple times more."

"No," Jones said.

"But you can't talk to a son-of-a-bitch like this."

Durell swung at Hackett again.

He was stronger now, and he felt the jarring impact of his knuckles on Hackett's mouth. Hackett crashed back against a tree, pushed away, and came at him. His eyes were pale, pleased crescents as he hit Durell in the stomach, face, and groin. Durell doubled forward and heard Jones's quick rebuke, but he knew that Hackett would not stop now. He struck back when he could, but Hackett did what he wanted with him.

chapter FIVE

HE WAS in a room in Washington, but he did not know where the room was, or the name of the street, or the quarter of the town he was in. The room told him nothing. It was a square cubicle with bare plaster walls and a set of government-issue office furnishings in oak: desk, armchair, swivel chair, two waiting chairs. Nothing on the walls. Tightly drawn green shades. A goose-neck lamp splashed light on the desk and into his eyes.

He was alone with Jones.

Jones said, lighting a cigarette, "What made you do it, Durell?"

"Maybe I was bored."

"Was it money?"

"I like money."

"A woman?"

"I like women."

"Do you like the Commies, too?"

Durell laughed, although it hurt his face.

Jones dragged at the cigarette. He was essentially a nice guy, Durell thought, one who was deeply disturbed, anxious, and upset about the apparent defection of a highly trusted agent.

"Hackett will be back," Jones said quietly. His eyes were fixed on the wall above Durell's head. "I wish you wouldn't try so damned hard to antagonize him. It won't buy you anything."

"What does Q have on you?"

"Nothing, thank God," Jones said quietly.

"Then why carry Hackett on your back?"

"Orders from upstairs. Quenton swings a big stick everywhere. He offers the staff a trained investigator like Hackett, checked out in every direction, and we have to accept him. Otherwise the papers scream, people get in trouble in mysterious ways, I'm out of a job, and when I look for another it's too bad, tough luck, no jobs available. So I tolerate Hackett."

"How long has it been going on?"

"Too long. I'm waiting for the real press to get the poop on it. Maybe it will end then. Until that time, I don't like it, you don't like it, nobody likes it. Quenton has himself a ball. Real patriot, our Texan. Rubs our noses in Texas dirt, makes us eat it." Jones looked at his cigarette. "Were you snowing me about Hackett doing the clobber job on you?"

"I don't think so."

"But you're not sure, eh?"

"No. I'm not sure."

"I almost wish it was true. That'd be a lulu. A real bozoom of a bust. I might look into it, though. It might mean a sharp knife slitting my throat. I must be nuts, but I like you, Durell."

"Thanks."

"I don't want any. Just don't get Hackett sore any more."

"Those Q men belong back in the Dark Ages," Durell said. "How does Quenton really get away with it—aside from turning everybody's innards green for fear they might get slapped with a subversive label by the almighty Quenton? Either you go along with Hereward, or you're a Red and a radical and a traitor, eh?"

"You've added two and two, brother."

"And where does Q keep his dirty files on our little government girls and top brass? That's where he twists the stick, right?"

"He has nothing on me. I live a clean, honest-to-God American life," Jones said, grinning a little.

"But where is the scandal buried?"

"Nobody knows," Jones said tiredly. "Are you all through?"

"I think Q stinks," Durell said. "Now I'm through."

Jones said in a different voice, "Yes. You are."

"Got enough on me to hang me?"

"Twice over."

"Let me talk to Dickinson McFee."

"He'll be here. Be patient."

"When?"

"Soon."

"I'll talk to him alone, or not at all."

"Sure."

"Not in this room, either."

"It's not bugged," Jones said.

"I don't believe anything you say. I'm sorry, Jones. You knuckle under to Q, and I don't think Quenton and his policy of fear ought to exist in our democracy. Quenton is taking a leaf out of the Nazi cookbook, and the brew he's stirred up is a stench in the nostrils of every decent American—or it would be, if folks knew about the atmosphere he's created here in Washington."

"I guess there's no use asking you what happened to the confidential file you stole."

"I don't have it," Durell said.

"But you admit you stole it?"

"I admit nothing."

"But you know where it is?"

"I'll talk to McFee."

Jones crushed out his cigarette and sat down behind the desk and stared at Durell with pale, disillusioned eyes.

He knew what fear was like. His fear was a deep, dark thing that crawled all through him as it grew. He had risked death many times to perform the assignments given him in the past, and he had never felt like this before. The fear was a sickness almost like claustrophobia, an insidious choking sensation as if walls were closing in on him, leaning over him, starting to topple down to crush him. His mind went over and over the path on which McFee had started him. He had been careless, perhaps. He had relaxed just once, for the first time, because Corinne was Sidonie's cousin and he was fond of Sidonie and Deirdre had been woven into it, somehow; and it was all a part of becoming attached to people, when you let them push and pull at you until you made one slip, let your guard down just once. Then you were through.

He did not know what time it was when McFee came into

the barren little room. He did not care. He stood up when Hackett opened the door and let the General enter.

"Not here," Durell said at once. "We won't talk here."

"It's all right, Sam," McFee said.

"How did Quenton get his gang of private snoops into a government affair? How do those buzzards get clearance, anyway? They act like tin gods, and I won't—"

"Relax, Sam."

"Get him out of here," Durell said. "Jones, too."

McFee looked at Hackett and Jones. Jones nodded quickly and started for the door. Hackett hesitated. His face was sullen; but he was unsure of himself. McFee's personality dominated him. He shrugged and went out.

"Sit down, Sam. Quenton is in on this. God knows how," McFee said wearily. "He's into everything, it seems. It's even worse than when he sat up on Capitol Hill and sabotaged everything and everybody from the White House on down in the name of the flag and the Lone Star State. I've been on the phone with him twice this morning. The Pentagon and Joint Chiefs, too. First time, I told Quenton to pull his cow hands off my range and keep them off. He didn't take it very kindly. That's when Joint Chiefs jumped me. Also two Senators. And State. *And* the White House, though damned if *they* seemed to like it. I had to be polite when Texas called the second time. Licked his nasty chops. He wants your head, Sam."

"Why?"

"You tell me."

They stared at each other in a moment's silence. McFee looked bitterly tired. There were dark shadows under his eyes, deep lines incised at the corners of his mouth. His gray suit was rumpled. Yet he carried himself with military precision, and his cool eyes had lost none of their keen perception. It seemed to Durell that Dickinson McFee looked at him with a remote and bleak reserve behind his words, as if he, too, had moved a step backward, away from him.

"How did Hereward Quenton know I had that file?" Durell asked.

"How does Q know anything? Money talks, and with some people, the more money you have, the louder you can talk. Quenton is dedicated to preserving a loyal government. That's his line. You can't quarrel with it. He has six or seven Senators on key committees riding with him. Have you ever met the man?"

"No."

"You're lucky, Sam. He's done some good work—give the devil his due. The Jennings case, the Freeland business. His men are tough, hard, good. Most departments are glad to accept 'em, especially when their salaries don't come out of the budget. That's one side of the coin."

"And the other?"

"Crackpot stuff. Lunatic-fringe groups. Hate Everybody cliques. He heads 'em all. No deals with the enemy, no peace conferences, let's A-bomb and H-bomb 'em off the face of this earth."

Durell waited.

"It's dangerous," McFee said. "Always dangerous, with that much money, that much press. They call Quenton the Baron of East Texas. Bigoted, narrow, rich, mean. So—dangerous."

"To us?"

"To all of us. You, me. Joe Corn in Iowa and Benny the Book on Times Square. All of us."

"Why don't we do something?"

"Not our job," McFee said. "The FBI keeps tabs on that sort of thing. We don't tread on their toes." The General shrugged. His face was cast in iron. "You asked how Quenton got onto the missing file. Nobody was supposed to know about it until we put the arm on you this morning and found it in your possession, right? But Quenton knew. Only one answer to it. Somebody in K Section works for him, of course. I didn't think they had managed to infiltrate us. But they have. You must admit they work fast and sure. They know everything about you on the cover plan; but they don't know, yet, about our private arrangement on this project."

"They won't learn about it from me," Durell said.

"All bets are off," McFee said flatly. "You may tell them if you wish."

"Will they believe me?"

"No."

Durell said, "What do you mean, all bets are off?"

"Give me the file you took, Sam."

Durell looked at him.

McFee said, "Are the Q men right? Did you lose it?"

"Yes."

"Who took it from you?"

"I don't know."

"You were with Corinne Ybarra?"

"Yes."

"Was she part of it?"

"I don't know."

"Were *you* part of it, Sam?"

The question came quietly, almost gently, but it was as if McFee had suddenly plunged a fist into his belly. Durell drew a deep breath, steadied himself, and met the General's bleak, ice-water eyes.

"Do you honestly think I've sold out?" Durell asked. "Do you think I'm playing a double game?"

"I'm not thinking. I'm asking."

"You know me better than to ask. Your question implies doubt."

"Don't be touchy, Sam. We're sitting on dynamite. Both of us. I'm not worried about myself. I've been around Washington a long time, and I know how the rules run in my echelon levels. But you're in trouble. It couldn't be worse. Do you understand?"

"No," Durell said flatly. "I don't."

"I can't help you," McFee said. "Not without that file. Give it to me, Sam, and then we can talk about what we can do."

"I don't have it."

"Look here. You're a good man, a careful man. You never slackened before, never left a chink in your armor. But tonight you let a fancy girl take you down the garden path to a mugging party. It doesn't sound like you. It doesn't ring true. Remember, I know you, Sam. Tough and suspicious and lonely. All right, you're going to get married. Did that addle your brains? Did you go with Corinne Ybarra like a trusting child?"

Durell said nothing. He had no answer. In some measure, what McFee said was true. Perhaps he had made a mistake in permitting Corinne to distract him for a vital moment. He had been perturbed about Deirdre, sick about the future. He had lowered his guard.

"Tell me what happened, Sam," McFee urged.

Durell told him. He made it brief and blunt, about Colonel Gibney, about the girl, the drive into Virginia, the chase and the manner in which he had been trapped. He watched McFee as he spoke, but the General's face never told him anything. He felt sick. McFee did not believe him. It was Mc-Fee's job to be suspicious, but he had not expected that suspicion ever to be directed against himself.

He felt the gray ugliness of being alone and friendless.

"Don't you believe me?" he asked McFee.

"It is not a question of believing or disbelieving. You had the file. I trusted you with it. You claim it's lost. It was your ultimate insurance against anything going wrong with your assignment. If you return it to me, we can go ahead with our project. Without it, the loyalty board has full authority."

Durell's mouth was dry. "They'll railroad me. You know how they work."

"Yes, I know."

"You're supposed to help me escape after the trial."

"That's out now."

"So I sweat it out alone?"

"In a federal penitentiary."

Durell stared in disbelief. "I can get the file back. I can get it back somehow."

"Through Corinne?"

"Maybe."

McFee said harshly, "She works for Quenton. You won't get it through her."

"Are you sure?"

"I'm not sure about anything that concerns Q. But I think she's the one. You're grabbing at a straw. Maybe Quenton is framing you, Sam. I don't know. Maybe you antagonized somebody over there."

"This is insane," Durell whispered. "Where is Corinne now?"

"She's disappeared."

"Did you check Colonel Gibney? He's soft on her."

"We've checked everything. She's off the face of the earth, as far as we're concerned. Maybe Quenton has her stashed away somewhere. Maybe she's off on her own little schemes. And maybe she's dead."

It was quiet in the little room. It was almost dawn, and he saw by the pale light that touched the window that there was only a blank brick wall beyond, perhaps six feet away. He got up and looked outside. An alley was below, too far down to jump, opening to a street fifty feet to the left. Dimly, the sounds of early traffic came to him. The morning was no cooler than the day just past.

He turned back to McFee, knowing he was pleading and making himself swallow his pride in order to plead. "I can find Corinne," he said. "I'll make her tell me the truth."

McFee shook his head. "You won't get the chance. You're under arrest. The loyalty board convenes at nine o'clock—four hours from now. It's all cut and dried. Your cell is waiting for you."

"And the rest of my assignment?"

"Canceled."

"I just go to jail?"

"That's the risk you took."

"You don't help me out?"

"I can't—unless you still have the file."

Anger flared in him. "Are you afraid of Quenton, too? Is that it, General? Does he have you scared and running? Does he frighten you so much that he can make you let me down, too?"

"I'm sorry," McFee said.

Durell sat down. He felt something change and harden and crystallize in him. He thought of many things: of the bayou country and his boyhood, of women he had known, of Deirdre and Lew Osbourn, of Sidonie and Corinne. They came to his mind in a ghostly parade, and as they appeared, he banished them, one by one, as if exorcising ghosts. He was alone. He did not need them or want them.

"What is it, Sam?" McFee asked in an odd voice.

Durell looked at him and did not reply.

McFee waited for a long moment, and again his face was of iron, his eyes of ice. Then he turned and went out.

chapter SIX

NIGHTMARE.

Six faceless men.

He heard the voice of the accuser: cold, contemptuous, certain. It was a single voice, repeated again and again, briefly and concisely hammering down the lid on the life and career of S. Durell.

The room was cool and official. There was no legend on the double-leafed door that led into it. There was a long polished table, scrupulously bare, and the row of identical chairs for the six identical faces of the members of this particular panel of the loyalty board. A male stenotypist sat with his back to the proceedings, near the heavy silken flags on their stands.

Durell listened to the accusations with a sense of detachment. He was here, but he was not here. He felt apart from what was happening here, as if nothing he did and nothing he said could matter.

"Mr. Durell, is it not a fact that you deposited twenty thousand dollars in the Capitol Bank and Trust Company yesterday, at approximately ten o'clock in the morning?"

"Yes," he said.

"The deposit was in cash?"

"Yes."

"Tell this board where you obtained that amount of money."

"No," he said.

"You refuse to answer the question?"

"I so refuse."

"On what grounds?"

"I plead the Fifth Amendment," he said.

The faceless men stirred as if a cool wind had blown among them. The chairman's voice grew more strident. "Did you obtain that money from gambling, Mr. Durell?"

"I have nothing to say about it."

"Is it not a fact that the money was, indeed, payment to you for carrying out certain espionage assignments detrimental to the welfare and safety of the United States of America?" Long, oratorical roll of voice, deep patriotic passion, anger rising out of justice and outrage. "Will you answer that question?"

"No."

"You will not say if it is true or false?"

"No."

"You are guilty of contempt, Mr. Durell. This board does not recognize any validity in the plea of self-incrimination contained in the Fifth Amendment, in this case."

Durell was silent.

There was a huddling of the six faceless men. It was quite hot and momentarily still in the official room. Durell's face ached. There was a dull pulse of pain over his eyes. He felt the weight of his outcast loneliness like the isolation of some dread quarantine. He felt the probe of coldly curious eyes in the white faces arrayed against him. He stirred restlessly. Despite all his previous mental adjustments, he sensed the blanket of guilt and shame that closed over him.

Nightmare.

McFee sat quietly, a small gray man of stone, his words like pebbles dropped into placid water, his eyes looking at and through the six faceless men.

Question: "Did you find Durell a capable, trustworthy operative in your department, General?"

"He satisfied all the tests. His past was thoroughly checked out. He was mentally and physically declared more than competent. He was brilliant."

Past tense, Durell thought.

"You had no slightest reason to doubt this man's loyalty?"

"None."

"Do you doubt it now?"

"Yes."

"Tell us why."

McFee spoke in a monotone. "We have reason to believe that he stole from confidential files not ordinarily accessible to him a series of dossiers on men who send us information from behind the Iron Curtain. These are invaluable men, whose data, you must understand, make up the basis for analysis and extrapolation of our opponents' industrial and social techniques. War potential today encompasses the whole community of a nation, the entire fabric of industry and technology. The secret agent is invaluable, but our section is composed mainly of technicians and scientists whose primary job is to analyze, deduce, and forecast enemy potentials in statistical form. Intelligence today is the fourth arm of our defense, gentlemen. The secret spy with confidential photographs is necessary, of course, but equally necessary are the men who have the capacity to interpret the meaning of those photographs."

"We understand. Just what did Durell do?"

"He has jeopardized the existence of an apparatus devoted to gathering for us material information. The apparatus consists of three men whose lives are now in imminent peril, if the documents Durell took from our files are not retrieved before they get abroad and into the wrong hands."

"And Durell has those documents?"

"He took them."

"He has them now?"

"I do not know."

"Why are you so certain, General, that this man is the guilty man?"

"I am only reasonably certain. My section is not devoid of its own apparatus for surveillance of its components."

"So you suspect Durell?"

"Yes."

"Of treason?"

"Yes."

"Would you say it is more than suspicion?"

"It is a ninety-per-cent certainty."

"If the people described in the missing dossiers are destroyed, if the men are executed or imprisoned, what damage will be done to our national security?"

"Perhaps very little. Perhaps it may prove decisive. We do not know. Those men will not be easy to replace. It may take six months or a year. It may never be possible to set it up again. The information we miss may be unimportant—or vital. Our work is cumulative, gentlemen. As I said, no single item of fact can be analyzed apart from its place in the entire structure of the nation from which it comes. War is total, destruction is total; information must be as close to totality as it is humanly possible to come, in order to assure ourselves of a chance for survival."

Mouths tightened. Eyes glistened. Faceless men, weighing, judging. And condemning.

Deirdre Padgett sat beside General McFee in a small, anonymous room in the undistinguished building where the loyalty-board trial took place. Durell stood with his back to the door, his dark eyes concealing shock. They had been given a brief recess, and there were guards on the other side of the door, and probably microphones in this bare little room. But he was beyond caring.

"Last chance, Sam," McFee said quietly.

Durell did not look at him. "Deirdre, did they call you back from New York?"

"It was Sidonie," she said, and the sound of her voice and the look of her and the feel of her presence in this room with his condemnation and shame made anguish rise in him. "She told me."

"You should never have come," he said.

"I had to. I wanted to."

He felt desperately weary. The hurt in her eyes was his hurt; the ugly thing that crawled behind the tremble of her mouth was an added knife twisting inside him. "It's only a trick, Deirdre," he said. "They want to make me break down and talk to you. As if I had anything to confess. They're using you, don't you see?"

"I don't care. Why won't you talk to me?"

"There's nothing to say."

She sat quietly, hands passively folded in her lap. It was a hot, sweltering day, yet she looked cool, with the freshness and immaculate sense of soap-selling cleanliness that he intimately remembered. She wore a white linen suit, and her long, firm-fleshed legs were crossed, and her hair was swept back like two delicate wings under a small flowered hat. Her gray eyes were fixed on him somberly, wide and enormous in her normally serene face. She wore net gloves and carried a red leather handbag, and her only accessory was a small golden lapel pin that he had given her one week end they had shared in New York. It had been in another time, another world.

"Last chance," McFee said again.

"Please, Sam. Tell him the truth," Deirdre said.

"Don't you think I've been telling the truth?"

"I don't know. Make me believe it," she said.

"Do I have to convince you?"

She looked at McFee.

"May we be alone?"

"No," said McFee.

"Please!"

"No."

There was a silence that stung and burned. Durell looked at McFee and saw no understanding, no clemency, no benefit of doubt. He looked at Deirdre. Her dark-gray eyes were enormous, with something growing in them as she met his gaze. She was beautiful. He wanted to cross the room to her and kneel before her and beg for her trust in him. He could not do it. The thing in her was growing and hardening, almost as if she leaned physically toward McFee.

Durell took a step toward the door. "Let's go back and get it over with."

"Where are the files, Sam?" McFee asked.

"I don't know. Where is Corinne?"

"No other answer for me?"

"None."

Deirdre said, "Sam, darling, why? If you love me—"

"Don't talk to me of love," he said harshly. "There's a time and a place for everything. Go back to New York. Forget about me. I did what I had to do, and it's over and done with. If I'm convicted at this phony trial, I go to prison for fifteen years. Will you wait for me?" he asked savagely. "Will you still love me then?"

She was shocked, her face whitening as if he had slapped her. She started to speak, then pressed her lips firmly together. A veil seemed to drop between them. She stood up with McFee.

"I'm sorry, General," she said. "If I could talk to Sam alone . . ."

McFee looked at Durell with bleak eyes. "I don't believe you could sway him. He hoodwinked me, and he can lie to you equally as well. I'm sorry, too. We'll go back."

Durell's mouth felt dry. "General . . ."

McFee stood with his head cocked slightly to one side. "We made a deal, McFee."

"It's off. I told you that."

"I get no help?"

"Not without those files."

McFee was almost to the door. Durell crossed the room while he waited to one side, and when he was abreast of the General he turned, pivoting on one foot, and chopped without warning at McFee with the edge of his palm against the General's neck. The blow was done quickly and expertly. It was completely decisive. Durell heard the girl gasp as McFee fell sidewise, eyes glazed and neural centers momentarily paralyzed. Durell hit McFee once more and McFee dropped. Durell caught him before his limp body thudded to the floor and lowered him without a sound.

Deirdre shrank to one side, staring wide-eyed at him.

"Sam . . ."

"Be quiet," he whispered harshly.

Her face was white and shocked. Durell listened for sounds of alarm from the corridor outside. There were none. Kneeling, he felt for McFee's pulse, flicked back an eyelid. It would be a few minutes before the General came to. The enormity of what he had done pressed up in him and he pushed it aside, thinking only of the moment, his mind jumping ahead only a step at a time. He looked at Deirdre again.

"Trust me," he whispered, straightening. "Please."

Her mouth shook. "Sam, they say you've been gambling, that you lost a lot of money, that you stole those things to pay off your debts. Is it true?"

"Yes. True. But not the whole truth. Will you help me?"

"I don't—"

He looked at her. In that moment he remembered how he had met her. She had good cause to know what it meant to be accused of treason; her brother had been similarly charged with betraying government secrets not long ago. He remembered how he had given her help against all of his training and instincts, believing in her as a fellow human in trouble and needing help. It seemed impossible that she could have forgotten this, or their love affair. He knew her intimately, every part of her. He loved her. He remembered her abandonment with him, the complete giving and sharing they had experienced.

"*Are* you guilty, Sam?" she asked.

"Would it make any difference?"

"I don't know. I feel relieved. Isn't that strange? Now I think I understand why you acted toward me the way you did."

There was no time to talk. He moved past her, sensing her perfume, feeling the feather-light touch of her hand as she reached impulsively for him, then withdrew. He listened at the door again. No sound. He did not know this house, this building, or where it might be located in the city. There could be a whole corps of guards outside. What he was trying to do might be utterly futile and damning. But he had to do it.

"Let's go," he said.

"You're going to escape?"

"I'm going to try."

He opened the door.

Immediately a tall, burly man standing outside in the empty corridor turned and stared at him with questioning eyes. Durell said quickly, "The General wants to see you."

He stepped back as if to return to the room. The guard hesitated, looked to the left, nodded to someone Durell could not see, and came forward. As he crossed the threshold, Durell hit him with all his strength, repeating the judo blow he had used on McFee. The man's neck was thick and strong. A grunt came from him and he fell to his knees, shaking his head, mouth strained open. Tight cords of muscle stood out in his throat. Durell shut the door. He waited until the guard had struggled halfway up again, then caught him with his knee under the chin and sent him flying backward to fall across one of the oak chairs. The crash seemed enormously loud in the empty room. The man was finished. Durell went over his clothes quickly, found the service revolver in its holster, checked the cylinder, and straightened with the gun in his hand.

Deirdre regarded him with wide, shocked eyes.

"Your turn now, Dee. Help me."

"Sam, I can't—"

"You go first."

She bit her lip, then moved to the door and opened it and walked out into the corridor. Durell followed. There was a crop-headed man to the left, near an intersecting hallway. The corridor had plaster walls painted green, with a tiled floor. Other doors on either hand were closed and gave no hint as to their purpose. The second guard spoke to Deirdre. "Are you with the General, ma'am?"

"Yes," Deirdre said. "He'll be right out."

The guard looked at Durell. "You going back to court?"

"Yes," Durell said. "I'm ready now."

"Where is Harry?"

"Inside with the General."

It was easy, Durell thought later. The guard looked in the office doorway and Durell struck at him with the gun he had taken from the first man. In a moment, he closed the door of the small conference room and stood alone in the hall with Deirdre.

She shrank away from him.

"I didn't know you could be so brutal," she whispered.

"Efficient, rather."

"What do you plan to do?"

"Get out of here. Get away from that loyalty board."

"They'll hunt you down. You'll never be free. You admit guilt by doing this, Sam. We'll both be forced to live like hunted animals for the rest of our lives."

He was surprised. "You're coming with me?"

"I want to," she said simply.

"You can't. I have to travel alone. But—thanks."

Her smile was a ghost, a wraith, fleeting and evanescent on her pale face. "I don't care what you've done, or why. I can't just—"

"Come on," he interrupted. "We haven't much time. Walk quietly with me and don't talk. Walk as if we have someplace specific to go. Are you afraid?"

"Not with you," she said.

They moved to the end of the corridor. Stairways with metal railings led down. They were on the third floor, and from up the stair well came the clatter of a lone typewriter in an office below. An elevator made a whining sound in the still, heavy heat. Deirdre's high heels tapped on the steel treads with determination.

They were in an office building, Durell guessed, of the sort that is leased quietly by the government for classified purposes. A fleeting image of the six faceless men who had judged him crossed his mind. There was still a residue of bitterness at the way McFee had deserted him, tossing him to the wolfish bigotry of the board and Quenton because their plan had failed. Well, he wouldn't be the fall guy for McFee or anyone else. An escape had been planned for him, and since the arrangements had been canceled, he would take this way to accomplish what had to be done. He knew that once in jail, he was through.

He paused on the landing above the street level. Deirdre halted a step above him, and he felt the slight pressure of her hand on his shoulder. He did not turn to look at her. He had changed. All his training of years past came to the surface now, and there was the deadly grace of a hunting animal in him, a sharpening of all his senses and a quickening of perception that made him at once dangerous, cunning, silent, and swift. He held the guard's gun with apparent carelessness. Street sounds came to him. He smelled Deirdre's fragrance along with the dust of the concrete walls of the stair well. How long before McFee or either guard revived? How long before a yell brought the house down?

Two men were talking just inside the entrance to the building. Hot sunlight made a yellow slab on the floor below, and he could see their elongated shadows just beyond the foot of the steps. And still no alarm from above. How much time did he have? The loyalty board would reassemble in a few minutes. They had been reluctant to give McFee any time at all for private conversation with him. He based his moves on a margin of five minutes, not much more or less.

"Sam, wait," Deirdre whispered.

He leaned forward, his hunter's head alert, the gun tipped up a little.

"Please don't go through with this," Deirdre whispered. "These men are your friends. You've worked with them. You can't use that gun."

"I have no friends." His voice carried only to the girl, and no farther. "You go down first, Dee."

"I can't do it. I thought I could, but I can't help you with any of this. It's wrong. If you're innocent—"

He looked at her, his dark-blue eyes almost black with stifled fury. "I'm not innocent. Do you understand that now?"

Although she did not move, he sensed the way she recoiled at his words. Her eyes were stricken, and he turned away. The two shadows on the sunlit floor were still below him.

"Go ahead," he said. "Go first, Deirdre. Distract them."

"No. I can't."

"Then you're with McFee. That right?"

"I want to be with you. But I can't do this, Sam!"

"All right. Stay here."

He went down the rest of the steps quickly and lightly, the gun dangling from his hand at his side. He took in the scene in the long, narrow lobby with one swift glance of comprehension. There were just the two men, standing ten feet inside the heavy glass doors. Hot sunlight made a glare on the busy street beyond. One of the men was Art Greenwald, short and burly, dark-haired, with thick brows over bright, witty eyes. He had worked with Art for several years; he had had dinner with Art and his wife, shared danger with him, spent time over drinks with him.

His gun came up.

He was halfway to the two men when Deirdre's voice rang out behind him.

"Sam, don't!"

Her cry of warning was like an accurately thrown knife, thudding into his back. The ultimate betrayal.

chapter SEVEN

ART GREENWALD looked at him for a moment of stunned lack of comprehension. The other man was someone Durell did not know, a lean military-looking man of middle age, with a hot flushed face in which the cheekbones stood out rubbed raw-red, either by the heat or by too much liquor. In the moment that Art hesitated, recognizing him, gathering in the meaning of Durell's appearance with a gun in his hand, Durell saved himself.

He shot Art neatly and accurately in the shoulder.

The bullet struck no higher or lower than he intended. The impact jolted Greenwald back against the wall and he went half spinning, knees buckled, fingers clawing at the concrete to keep himself erect. On his face was a look of utter incredulity.

The sound of the shot echoed in the bare lobby like a pistol fired into a metal barrel.

Durell jumped forward, hearing Deirdre call his name again. He did not look back. The second man with Greenwald was reaching clumsily into his pocket, his face red with hate and anger. Durell hit him across the cheek with the flat of his gun, and as he went down, he spun past him and stiff-armed the heavy swinging doors and ran out into the street.

The heat and sunlight struck him, blinded him. He halted. A woman began to scream from inside the building. Not Deirdre. A man shouted hoarsely. There was some traffic on the street, and he saw a row of shops mixed with small, shabby office buildings, and he ran across the asphalt to the shade on the opposite pavement. A passer-by got in his way and he bowled the man over, spun on his heel, and ducked into a haberdashery. The clerk looked up, startled, frozen behind the glass counter. The shop was air-conditioned. The clerk saw Durell's gun and his gesture and pointed to the back door. Durell slammed through into a storeroom, a cluttered office, another doorway, an alley. He turned to the right, running hard through the smothering heat. At the mouth of the alley he put the gun away. The second street was wider, busier. A trolley came rocking along and he considered it, abandoned it, and ducked around it. There was a traffic cop at the corner. There was a sound of sirens behind him. The cop saw him running and blew a whistle. Durell twisted around the corner, dodged through a crowd of shoppers. A clock over a jewelry store read just noon. That was in his favor. Ahead were some government buildings, just beginning to disgorge their office workers for lunch. He ran that way, crossed another broad avenue, and slowed to a walk.

He was drenched, soaked through with sweat. The hot summer air was like glue in his throat, his lungs. A police car slammed by, threading in and out of traffic. The voices of female government clerks and stenos filled the air with a birdlike chattering. He forced himself to walk more slowly. Only a few curious glances came his way. Another police car screamed by. At the following corner he paused and looked back. He saw no one chasing him on foot.

He found a hack stand, gave the cabby a five-dollar bill for the privilege of having the cab unshared, and told the driver to take him to the Pentagon.

An hour later he sat in a bar in downtown Alexandria, drinking rum and Coke. It was an old-fashioned taproom, not crowded. There was fine smoky paneling and big wooden fans that circulated the humid, beery air through the place. The bartender was intent on the television screen, broadcasting a ball game. Durell had changed cabs in the maze of the Pentagon, crossed back to Pennsylvania Avenue, picked up a bus that went past his apartment. He saw enough to know it was watched and guarded. He did not get off.

Now he was faced with a temporary freedom that offered him no good purpose. His mind, trained to think with incisive clarity, seemed clogged by useless emotional reactions. He told himself not to think of Deirdre's betrayal or McFee's desertion. He tried to wipe out the picture of Art Greenwald's face when he shot him. It was not easy. It is never easy to be entirely alone. There had been a time when he needed no one, wanted no one. Something had happened to him after he first met Deirdre. He had compromised with his convictions, lost some of his self-reliance, and this had taken something from him that he needed once again. He had to have it back, or he was lost. He would never survive.

All through the city, and beyond, he knew they were hunting for him. A hundred men, a thousand men, in uniform and out, all searching with only one objective. Find Sam Durell.

Dead or alive.

He knew that would be the order. He'd have given the same order himself, in Burritt Swayney's spot, or in McFee's position.

Find him. Bring him back. Or kill him.

There would be panic in some quarters, cold dismay in others. He knew too much. The Joint Chiefs, the Pentagon, the FBI, and Atomics would be in the worst flap of the year.

The bartender came over and said, "Another, mister?"

"Yes. The same."

"You feel all right, mister?"

"Just fine."

"You look like you could use some sleep."

"Thanks," Durell said. "Maybe I'd better. Skip the drink."

He got up, paid, and went out. He felt haunted.

Corinne, he thought. She has the file. Or she knows where it is.

He found a small tailor's shop first, had his suit pressed, the torn pocket repaired. It took half an hour. He used the time to sit quietly and think. When his clothing was returned, somewhat more presentable than before, he found a drugstore, a phone booth, and dialed the number of Sidonie Osbourn's office at Number 20 Annapolis Street.

A long chance. Dangerous. But it had to be taken. There was no other choice.

Sidonie answered. Durell spoke at once. "Sid, are you being tapped?"

There was a moment's stunned silence. Then, "No. I don't think so. Where are you?"

"Don't mention my name. It doesn't matter where I am."

"Of course not. Sorry I asked." Strain ran through her voice like tightly corded muscles. "Are you all right?"

"So far. But I must talk to you."

"I don't think you should."

"You're the only one, Sidonie. I need help. There's nobody else. Please."

"All right. Where?"

"Your house," he decided. "Where are the twins?"

"I'll be home before the children show up. But I can't promise that I won't be followed. I'll be as careful as I can."

"Is Swayney at his desk?"

"He's in conference at the White House. You can imagine why."

"You're alone?"

"Yes."

"Where is Corinne?"

"Nobody knows. They're still looking for her."

"Can you help?"

She was silent.

"Can you tell me?"

"Not now. Hang up. I'll see you soon."

There was a click, and silence. Durell cradled the phone, sat still for a moment, feeling the sweat on the back of his neck. All at once his mind began to function again on clear, level lines, closing on his plan like the snap of a trap. One avenue was open to him. Perhaps the only way out. He knew the odds against him. It was his business to know the odds. He had perhaps half a day, maybe a full day of freedom—given luck, given the use of all the arts, wiles, and stratagems he knew how to employ. Sidonie might be a snare. He had to risk that, because he saw no other way to reach out for Corinne. And he needed Corinne. She was his only tangible point of reference on the road back.

He sat in hot, silent shadows, waiting. He sat without moving, using patience that conquered the quick, twisting cramp of muscles, the dragging passage of time.

Sidonie was late.

Her house, in one of the mushroom developments outside of Alexandria, was one of a row of identical Cape

Cods, on a quiet curving street of raw new lawns struggling to survive in the August sun. The sounds of children at play came from the far end of the street. A laundry truck, an occasional tradesman, a housewife going shopping made up the only traffic. There was a safe, sleepy atmosphere to the neighborhood, a sense of peace and security and comfort. Sidonie's house was a third of the way up from the corner. Durell had taken a local bus to within three blocks, and walked the rest of the way. He had looked for signs of a stakeout, not underestimating Swayney or McFee. Nobody had been watching Sidonie's house. When he entered by the unlocked screened porch in the rear, he had kept the gun ready for a trap. But there was no trap. It made him uneasy, this apparent lack of efficiency in the forces lined up against him.

He waited, seated in an armchair in the tidy little living room where he had spent many evenings with Lew and Sidonie before Lew was killed. The heavy draperies over the picture window facing the street were drawn against the western sun. The room was almost dark, and still Sidonie did not come.

A sedan rolled down the street, slowed in front of the house almost imperceptibly, and went on. Its horn sounded briefly at the distant corner. Durell did not move. The gun was quiet in his lap.

A small clock with Roman numerals, set in a polished walnut cabinet, ticked steadily in the oppressive heat. From the top of the spinet piano, Lew's photo smiled at him, set in a silver frame. A child wailed on the lawn opposite the house. The car turned the corner and came drifting slowly back, then went on with a quick burst of speed.

He did not move.

She did not come.

He remembered a time like this in the bayou, when he was a boy, with his grandfather. They were hunting a small herd of pigs gone wild—mean, vicious animals that would kill if given the chance. The old man knew their rooting grounds, down below a crumbling *chenière,* and he had taken Durell, the boy, with him, with their guns. All day long they had hidden in the wild oleander brush and waited. The afternoon had been a torment of heat and insects and still, deathly silence. The old man taught him what patience meant, both to the hunter and to the hunted. One of many lessons, Durell thought now, remembering the flies that bit him, the smell of the swamp's brackish water, the brilliance of water hyacinth floating still on the dark bayou—and always the old man, until the gun was miraculously at his shoulder, and the crack of the .30-30 echoed high and quick, along with the grunt and crash and death of the wild boar.

She did not come.

He waited, wondering now what would happen if the twins came home first. He did not want to involve Sidonie in his own trouble. It would go badly for her if he were seen here. He was sure none of the neighbors had spotted him. But the twins would talk, innocently enough, and damn Sidonie and himself. He wondered about the car that had twice passed the house. A sense of pressure began to grow in him, a feeling of being encircled, trapped. Sidonie might betray him. Nothing was impossible. You can't trust anyone now. They know you're sitting in here, waiting. They can afford to tighten the net until there isn't any loophole left for you to get through. And they know you, Durell thought. They're a little afraid of you. They won't close in until they're sure.

They.

He stood up all at once, his body light and poised and graceful for his size and weight. A big man, heavily muscled, Durell was able to drift like a shadow in utter silence toward the front door.

Then the screened door at the back of the house clicked and he heard the quick tap of high heels on the porch floor. He turned, the gun up. He waited. Sweat trickled down the back of his neck.

"Sam, I'm sorry."

It was Sidonie Osbourn.

Behind her was Deirdre.

chapter EIGHT

SIDONIE CLOSED the door quietly, but the click sounded loud and sharp in the hot stillness. She smiled, but it did not touch her eyes. Small, petite, delicate, she stood where she was for a long moment, a trim little woman whose adult face was shadowed by past tragedy that she had overcome. Deirdre stood taller, copper-haired, looking at Durell's gun.

"Put it down," she said quietly. "Or would you use it on me as you used it on Art, your friend?"

Her words cut and slashed at him.

"Are you two alone?" he asked.

"We didn't bring anyone along," Sidonie said quietly. "We've been careful. You look awful, Sam. I don't like the way you look."

"It's the way I feel. Why did you bring Deirdre?"

"She wants to talk to you."

"It's all been said. There's nothing else to talk about."

"Sam," Deirdre began, then paused. She drew a breath, came a step toward him, paused again. A pleading touched her mouth and her eyes. "I didn't cry out to betray you back there. I know that's what you're thinking. I just couldn't help myself, that's all. I thought you were going to kill Art Greenwald."

"How is he?" Durell asked flatly.

"It's a shoulder wound. It's not serious. Please believe me, Sam. Sidonie and I both came here to help you, in any way we can. We can't guess what you're planning to do, but if we can help to clear you, we want to do whatever we can."

He remained standing in silence, while Sidonie pulled off her white gloves and put aside her handbag. Deirdre sat down, her back straight, her mouth defensive. He went to the window and pulled the drapery apart an inch and looked out at the hot glare of the residential street. Nothing. Nothing he could see, anyway. But that didn't have to mean anything. He said, addressing Sidonie, "I just want to know where I can find your cousin Corinne."

"Why do you want to find her?" Sidonie whispered.

"Because she's in it, too."

"I can't believe that."

"She is."

The small girl shook her head. Her eyes were shadowed, and she looked at Durell for a moment without understanding. "You don't know Corinne, really. She had a bad time, long ago. She was just a youngster during the war, when France was occupied. My uncle—her father—was killed, and she—the German troops—they used her. She got away into Spain and lived in Barcelona. It was necessary for her to use anything she could, in order to survive. When Lew helped me find her and bring her over here, she seemed to settle down and was very quiet for a time. Then she became—as you know her now."

"Where is she?" Durell asked bluntly.

Sidonie folded her hands. Her small teeth bit her under-lip. She did not look like the mother of twin ten-year-olds. She looked like a child herself.

"How can she help you, Sam?"

"The less you know, the better. Is Swayney still looking for her?"

"Yes."

"Have they pulled in Colonel Gibney?"

"Who?"

"The colonel I've been dealing with. You've been right in the office with McFee and Swayney. You know what line they're taking. If you want to help me, tell me what they're doing and what they're planning to do, so I can be prepared."

"I can't do that," she said quietly. She lifted her eyes to meet Durell's hard gaze. She winced at the look on his face. "I can't betray the trust they have in me, or the job I do. Not like that. Not even for you, Sam."

"Then tell me where I can find Corinne. You know, don't you?"

"Will you hurt her, Sam?"

He could have lied. But he told her the truth. "I don't know. I may have to kill her."

Deirdre made a small, shocked sound. Durell saw her face close against him in protest, rejecting his statement. It couldn't be helped. He stood with his feet slightly spread, aware of the two girls watching him and hesitating, yet with all his senses tuned for any sign of a trap outside.

"Corinne is just wild, Sam," Sidonie whispered. "She couldn't be guilty of anything serious. She's free and en-joying life for the first time. She's abusing her freedom, it's true, but she is sure to settle down. She had to fight so hard once, simply to survive! She cannot be a traitor to this country that's given her peace and safety for the first time in her life."

He leaned forward a little. "You haven't told Swayney or McFee where she is, but you know. You're protecting her."

"I'm protecting you, too," she protested.

"Which one of us will you help?" he demanded.

She said despairingly, "I want to help you both. I want to help Deirdre, who loves you. Can't you see what a nightmare this is to me, Sam? I love all of you, too. I don't want anyone hurt. And I want so much to be sure that I make no mistakes. I don't want to do the wrong thing."

"Make a choice," he said. "I have to talk to Corinne. It's important to me. Nothing could be more important. She has what I need to clear myself."

Deirdre said quickly, "You said you were guilty, Sam."

"I can't explain any more of that."

"But Corinne *can* help you?"

"She's the only one."

He waited. He felt Sidonie's indecision and understood it and waited for the pendulum to swing. He could have pleaded with her in other ways; he could have demanded her loyalty as payment for things he had done for Lew in the past. But he couldn't bring himself to set a price like that for her.

The length of the room separated him from Deirdre. She had not come close to him, she had not touched him; but her troubled eyes never left his face, seeking an answer to what she could not understand. He had hurt her deeply. Perhaps it was too much to expect her to trust him, he thought, but he felt the galling disillusionment of her retreat from him. There should have been no hesitation in her, if she loved him as he had hoped. His mind felt remote and cool and distant from all this, however. At this moment, he was both the hunter and the hunted, all in one.

Then at last Sidonie said, "Corinne telephoned me."

"Your phone is tapped," he countered harshly.

"I know. Before she said anything to give herself away, I switched the call to McFee's private line. He was out. I took the chance someone might come in."

"McFee could be tapped, too."

She looked helpless.

He waited, watching her.

"Corinne wants to see you, Sam."

"Is that what she said?"

"You're to go to a town called Locust Grove. It's on the Virginia state highway to Cramden Beach. Do you know it?"

"I can find it." There were rumors about the colony at

Cramden, the decadent entertainment run for a certain type of high brass. "I've never been there."

"You're not to go anywhere but Locust Grove. At Bailey's Drugstore, ten o'clock sharp. Someone will meet you there."

"Not Corinne?"

"Someone. That's what she said."

"It sounds melodramatic."

"She was frightened. The police are looking for her, too. Every police agency of the country, Sam. For you and for Corinne. It's on the radio already. In another hour it will be splashed across all the evening papers."

"What are they calling me?"

She bit her lip.

"Say it, Sidonie."

"A traitor," she whispered.

He looked at Deirdre. She looked away.

"Are you, Sam?" Sidonie asked.

He said roughly, "The less you know about it, the better. Thanks for your help."

"I don't want to believe it. Make me *not* believe it!"

"I can't," he said heavily.

"But it's so senseless! *Why*, Sam?"

"Tell me the rest about Corinne."

"That's all she said. She pleaded with me not to speak about her call to anyone but you. I couldn't make up my mind. I didn't promise her that I'd give you the message. And then she hung up, all at once. I hope I've done the right thing."

His mind probed at the problem. A trap? Not from the police. The police could have taken you right here, if Sidonie had chosen to speak to them. More of the people who stole the file? Maybe. Should you walk into it? Yes. What could you lose?

You could die.

"Thank you, Sid," he said gently. "I'm grateful."

He put his gun away inside his coat.

"You will have to leave now," she told him. "The children are due home at any minute. They shouldn't see you here."

"I know."

"Deirdre?" Sidonie said.

Durell swung to look at her. There was an ache in him, a brief claw of remembered desire as he watched the grace with which she moved and heard the soft timbre of her voice.

"I bought a car this afternoon," she told him. Her eyes met his evenly. "It's parked two blocks away. The key is under the floor mat. It's for you, Sam. There's money in the dash compartment. Two hundred dollars. It was all I had left. I don't know if you need more or not. I can get more for you tomorrow. But I thought you might not be here tomorrow. The car can take you to Mexico or the other side of the world, eventually—if that's where you want to go."

"I'm not running away," he said, looking at her with a new wonder. He had thought of her as betraying him, and now she had given him this gift of trust and help. He felt oddly confused, still not accepting her with that cool, calculating part of his mind that had come to the fore. "I'll use the car. Thank you, Deirdre."

Sidonie got up and went toward the kitchen. "I think it will be all right if you stay another few minutes, Sam."

He was alone in the room with Deirdre.

He felt the awkward lack of words to say what was needed. Words were inadequate. Then he saw the way her face changed, tightening and closing against him.

"You still don't believe in me, do you?" he asked softly.

"I don't know what to believe. I love you. But now I'm mixed up about everything. I always thought of you as something to be depended on. For eternity. So strong, so straight. Now I don't know what to think."

"Why help me, then?"

"I don't know." She shrugged. "Perhaps because Sidonie is willing to believe in you and risk everything. Perhaps she makes me feel guilty and ashamed of not helping, too. I still think you have no right to fight this the way you're doing. I still think you should give yourself up and trust to justice to give you a fair deal."

"To the loyalty board?"

"I don't know anything about it. To McFee."

"McFee has to knuckle under to them. To the Q people. You've heard of Quenton?"

She nodded. "Is Quenton that bad?"

"Worse than bad. It may be the worst treason that can be committed. Treason in the name of loyalty and patriotism. I can't stomach it. I have to fight it. I think it may be more important than my own small, personal problem."

She turned away. "I bought the car secondhand. It's a green Chevrolet coupe, registered in my name. The title registration is in the glove compartment." At the kitchen door she faced him. "Will you take me with you, Sam?"

"Why should you want to go?"

"I just want to be with you. We were together once before, when my brother stood where you're standing now. You helped me then. Let me help you now."

"You don't owe me anything," he said. "Don't do it out of any sense of obligation."

He saw the hurt in her and he wanted to cry out that nothing he said now was to be accepted as the whole truth; he wanted to explain how he had to push her aside, to save her from whatever catastrophe came his way. He saw no other choice. If he told her the truth, she would insist on joining him. And he could not risk that.

Her mouth trembled. "All right, Sam. You're alone. That's the way you want to be, isn't it? Good luck."

The misunderstanding lay like a vast, dark ache between them as he went out.

chapter NINE

HE TOOK TIME to call Art Greenwald's home from a drugstore in a small wayside town deep in the tidewater country. The Greenwalds lived in a crowded apartment just outside Washington. Rosalie was a dark-haired, buxom girl with born vivacity, and her mother lived with them, a quiet woman of Orthodox piety. On the occasions when Durell had spent an evening there, they had casually drawn him into the warm, close circle of their intense family relationships.

Rosalie answered the phone.

"Rose, are you alone?" he asked.

"Who is this?" There was sudden strain in her soft, pleasant voice. "Who is talking?"

"Sam. Do you have company?"

"Oh, you son-of-a-bitch," she said quietly.

"I just want to know how Art is doing."

"After you shot him?"

"Rosalie, I couldn't help it. I had to."

Shocking hatred shook her voice, which he remembered as warm and laughing and companionable. "You have your nerve, to call here after what you did! And what you're doing. It's not just shooting Art. It's everything else, you bastard. Art loved you. He thought you were great. You know what he did this afternoon when they brought him home? He cried. I never saw him cry before, not even when Sissie was sick and almost died. He cried for you, you rotten—"

She broke off and he heard the silence and felt the hating. Voices argued dimly in the receiver.

He felt uneasy.

Then Art was on the line. "Sam? Thanks for placing the slug in my shoulder. No bone hit."

"I'm sorry about it, Art."

"Don't mind Rosalie. She's upset, you understand. I wouldn't stay in the hospital. But, you Cajun maniac, I know you could have put that slug between my eyes. I know how you can score."

"Art, is your wife calling on another phone to trace me?"

"Sam, tell me something."

"Is she?"

"Listen, Sam, I don't care what they say about you—"

"Thanks."

He hung up and left the booth and the town fast. But no matter how fast he drove, he could not run away from the echoes of hatred and contempt in Rosalie's voice, riding with him.

It was twenty minutes to ten when he reached Locust Grove. Bailey's Drugstore was not difficult to find. Aside from the marquee of the movie house, its sign was the only light still shining on the dusty main street. He drove past it. Cars were parked in diagonal slots up and down in front of the movie house. They looked empty. One of them could shelter men waiting in ambush, crouching on the floor. He found a parking slot at the end of the line and got out carefully and walked with even more care up the empty sidewalk. His heels made hollow sounds on the brick pavement. There were no police. The cashier's booth under the marquee was empty. Moths fluttered in bright silence against the street lamps and the druggist's window. Durell walked by. At a glance, the place looked empty. There was nothing unusual about it. A soda fountain, prescription counter, cosmetics, magazines, garden tools. Crickets shrilled in the field behind the shop. He turned and went in.

No Corinne.

He ordered a Coke from the sleepy-eyed boy behind the fountain, and while he drank it he saw his face jump at him from the rack of newspapers nearby. He did not bother to buy any of the papers. He looked at the soda clerk. The boy chewed gum, slowly and methodically, popping it with quiet regularity.

Ten o'clock.

Nothing and nobody.

Then the telephone in the rear booth began to ring.

Pop! The boy chewed his gum, watching him. *Pop! Pop!*

The phone rang with shrill persistence, muffled inside the booth. The clerk leaned both hands on the soda counter.

"Ain't you gonna answer it, mister?"

"What makes you think it's for me?"

"The dame said you'd be here for a call at ten o'clock. She's right on the button." *Pop.* "Wish Sarah-Ellen was on time like that."

Durell looked at the boy and read nothing to alarm him in the freckled, sleepy face. He slid off the stool and went to the booth, looked back at the drugstore door, saw nobody there, and picked the receiver off the hook.

"Yes?" he said.

She was breathless. "Sam? Is that you?"

"Yes, Corinne."

"Thank God Sidonie decided to give you the message. Are you all right?"

"That depends. No, I'm not all right."

"I mean—are you alone? Free?"

"Alone. Not free."

"Oh, please. Darling, I want to help you."

"You've done plenty to me, Corinne. I thought you'd be the last to want to help."

"Don't be suspicious. Please. I couldn't stand that, after taking this chance. It's in all the newspapers about you, Sam. It's awful. I don't understand why you did it, but I don't care. I just don't care." Her voice went on and he looked through the booth doors at the clerk who chewed gum and at the dark street beyond the door. The booth smelled of stale tobacco and dead perfume. He sweated. Corinne's voice trailed off. "Are you listening?"

"Where can I see you?"

"That's just it. They're not quite sure of you. They made me set this up, Sam, and they don't know I'm calling. Keep watch for them. If they come in, hang up quick."

"Who?"

"Amos Hackett is coming to the drugstore for you," Corinne said.

He felt cold. "Hackett?"

"He's with the same people I work for. He'll take you to where it's safe. I know it sounds crazy to you, and Hackett didn't want to, but when he heard that you really shot Art Greenwald, one of your best friends, he became convinced. He said you were tough and tricky, Sam, and he still doesn't trust you."

"It sounds as if I've joined a club," he said flatly.

"Yes. Yes, Sam."

"The same you belong to?"

She paused. Her voice faded. "Yes."

He watched the door. Moths flickered and danced around the lights. A car went by, dim and silent on the village street.

"Corinne?"

"Go with Hackett when he comes for you," she said quickly. "Don't argue with him. You will be *safe*."

"Safe—with Hackett?"

"I promise you. Yes. But don't talk to him, don't say anything to him or anyone else, until I see you first. That's why I'm taking this chance—calling you, I mean. Meet me on the beach."

"What beach?"

"There's a beach here. There's to be a swimming party tonight. To the right of the house—south of it, I think— there's a big sea wall. I'll be waiting for you there. Don't discuss anything with them until we've talked. It's important, darling. To both of us. Get on the beach somehow, as soon as you can." She gave a nervous, shocking giggle. "It's some party. Like nothing you ever saw before. You'll see what I mean."

"Corinne, where are you?"

"Hackett will bring you here. Remember. The sea wall."

"Corinne, do you have that file?"

"No, I don't," she said calmly.

She hung up.

He stared at the dead phone, replaced the receiver with

meticulous care, opened the booth door, and looked at the entrance to the drugstore.

Hackett had come for him.

The thin man stood in part shadow, and there was a difference in him, perhaps in the assurance he carried in him, or in the quietly expensive clothes he wore. Durell was not certain. There was the same dark lock of hair over the flat forehead, the long nose, the conspiratorial flash of clever eyes in that thin face. There was arrogance in him and intelligence, mingled with arrant brutality that Durell already knew.

The wide, narrow mouth smiled.

"Take it easy," Hackett said quietly.

They looked at each other across the width of the store like two jungle animals.

"Come with me," Hackett said. "Easy does it."

Pop.

They both glanced at the soda clerk. The boy shrugged and picked up a comic book and sat down, paying no more attention to them. Durell walked from the booth to the doorway. Hackett's hands were in plain sight.

"Did the girl call you?" Hackett asked.

"Yes."

"Then you understand."

"Not entirely."

"It will be explained. Let's go to my car."

Durell went out on the sidewalk with him. The main street of Locust Grove was still empty, but the lights on the movie marquee had been put out, and the cashier's booth was curtained and dark. From far away came the rumble of a Diesel truck on the main highway.

"After you," Durell said.

The car was a small red Austin-Healey with monogrammed initials on the door and an insigne that looked like a silver cattle brand, but Durell could not be sure. Hackett got behind the wheel; Durell slid to the black leather seat beside him. His nerves tightened, plucked at his bones. Hackett smelled of rum and shaving lotion.

"You understand," the man said, "I had to rough you up when Jonesy was there. It was front. I don't apologize for it."

"You enjoyed it," Durell said.

Hackett nodded. "I don't like you. I don't trust you. But I follow orders. They told me to bring you in, so we'll go."

"They?"

"You'll see."

"Suppose the cops stop us on the way?"

"It's a good chance. Then you're under arrest, in my custody. The thing blows up. I may have to shoot you, but I'd have to slit my throat doing it, too. They won't stop us, though."

"You're sure of yourself."

"We have influence."

"Where are we going?"

"Cramden Beach."

"And what's there for me?"

"Safety. No cops. *If* you play ball. Personally, I hope you get hot and stubborn. I'd like to handle you."

"Why should you want anything with me? You've got the file. You took it from me long before you came back with Jones."

"No."

"Don't play games, Hackett."

"No. There's no point in our talking. You willing to go?"

"Sure," Durell said.

There was satisfaction in him, a knowledge that he had set his feet on the right path. Where it would eventually lead was of no concern just now. Some of his depression and defeat lifted from him. He had made contact. For good or evil, thanks to the bullet he had slammed into Art Greenwald's shoulder, he had succeeded in convincing those needing to be convinced that he was a man without a country, a fugitive from the police arm of the government. What loomed ahead seemed infinitely bigger than anything he or McFee had anticipated at the start. It would not be easy. Death lay ahead if he took a wrong step, if his tongue slipped. But he had been down this road before. And others had gone before him, in other times. Not all had returned. Maybe he, too, would not return. He told himself not to be surprised by Hackett's new role as part of a subversive group. He was trained not to prejudge or anticipate too much toward a conclusion. Something big was going to happen. He could feel it.

Let it come, he thought.

He shifted slightly on the leather seat, so the gun in his pocket was more readily available.

chapter TEN

THEY DROVE in silence for most of an hour before the car rumbled over a wooden bridge that spanned a salt-water creek. In a few moments they came to another bridge. Lighted windows glimmered to the south, along the narrow sand road that led the length of the island. It was cooler here, and the air was brisk with the smell of the sea. Hackett turned right and he caught the white glimmer of long, plumed combers rolling up out of the black Atlantic. The crash and boom of the surf entered the car with the pungency of the salt sea wind. Hackett slowed. They passed several wooden beach cottages, all dark, shuttered. It was ten minutes before midnight.

Strips of white-painted wood barricaded the road ahead. The shapes of two men loomed suddenly in the Austin-Healey's headlight, and Hackett stopped. The two men approached the car. They wore dark, sober clothes and their faces were polite, curious, and guarded.

"That you, Amos?"

"It's all right, Tom," Hackett said through the window.

"No trouble, hey?"

"None of your goddamn business," Hackett said. "Lift the gate. The mainland cops haven't been around?"

The man, obviously a guard, laughed softly. He never looked at Durell. "I see you got the package. All we got are the guests. It's another wing-ding down the beach. All that skin. I wish I had the binoculars."

"Try it and you'll get reamed."

"Well, I wish I was borned rich instead of handsome."

"Lift the gate," Hackett said.

His voice had softened, but there was a cold quality of authority and command. The guard looked surprised and then uncomfortable.

"Sure thing, Amos. I was only kidding."

"Mr. Hackett," Hackett said.

73

"Yes, sir, Mr. Hackett."

"How many men are posted?"

"Seven. Beach to beach."

"All right. Don't bother scratching sand fleas. Keep your eyes open. No unauthorized people tonight, hear?"

"Yes, sir. Don't get sore, Mr. Hackett."

The gate was opened and the Austin-Healey drove on through. The road immediately grew wider and less bumpy. Durell lit a cigarette. "You're well organized. Private cops?"

"Official police of the town of Cramden Beach. I happen to be the chief."

"What's the population?"

"About ten," Hackett said, grinning.

"Lots of cops."

"Money will buy anything," Hackett said. "The souls of men, anything. It will buy you, too."

"I wouldn't mind," Durell said, "if there were enough of it."

"There's enough, provided you've got what we want."

"The file?"

"Nothing else."

"But you've got that," Durell said.

"You stupid Cajun. Do you think you'd be here if we had it?"

"Maybe you're keeping it for yourself, for a private deal."

Hackett's lean head turned sharply. His face was angular and bony in the shadows. His white eyes gleamed, his teeth shone. "More of that talk, and you'll look down and find yourself dead."

"Hit home?"

"Swung and missed."

"You say."

The car slowed perceptibly. "Can we make a deal?" Hackett asked quietly.

"Cold cash?"

Hesitation. "Yes."

"For the file?"

"Yes."

"I don't have it," Durell said, and laughed.

"You son-of-a-bitch," Hackett whispered softly.

The car lurched ahead again.

A picnic fire gleamed far ahead on the barren dunes. The change from Washington's humidity made Durell feel better. His thoughts ranged ahead clearly and quickly. They passed a large house with a single lighted window, shielded from the primitive road by twisted shrubbery and a palisade fence. Then the roof of a yet larger house lifted black against the silvered ocean, and their headlights flickered on another barrier and more guards. They were passed through a tall gateway and Hackett parked at the end of a long line of cars in the shell drive.

Hackett got out of the Austin-Healey. "Keep your nose clean. Don't twist your neck too much. You're only on probation. Use your mouth loosely, and we blow the whistle on you. McFee would like to take you apart piece by piece."

Durell stared at the house. It was enormous, a pattern of stone and glass and light that looked as if it had been fashioned out of the sea and land together. Long and low, it held a resemblance to a Western ranch house of the more sumptuous order, and at first he was struck by the incongruity of its presence on a wild Virginia beach. Then he saw how the architect had radically fashioned the huge structure out of native elements so that the house seemed to be a part of the beach and a part of the sea, with long wings reaching toward the surf, a higher central body with clerestory windows lifting from the dunes toward the rear. As he walked with Hackett to a side entrance, through clipped lawns and trim shrubbery, he glimpsed a patio and a tall woven fence that cut off his view of the beach itself. To his right was a sea wall that made a long black line of shadow against the brighter shine of the surf. He glanced at the sea wall again and did not see Corinne and glanced away.

The surf sounded with muffled thunder beyond the fence, and above the crash of the combers came the varied strains of music. The cars in the driveway were rich and powerful: a white Jaguar, three MG's, a Lancia, several Cadillacs with official government licenses. Durell's mouth tightened. Above the music in the house came snatches of conversation and laughter pitched just a shade too high, tight with a hysterical gaiety.

Hackett crossed the patio with a long stride. The gate in the beach fence was opened to admit a white-jacketed waiter carrying a tray of empty glasses, and Durell glimpsed the beach beyond. Around a picnic fire were gathered half a dozen people, men and women sprawled in the ruddy glare and the softer moonlight. It apparently was a nude swimming party. He caught only a snatch of the scene, and then the door closed and the waiter crossed the patio softly ahead of them, nodding with respect to Hackett.

"This way," Hackett said. His flat voice and thin face registered contempt for what he saw.

Durell had halted. Within the house, seen through tall glass windows facing the ocean, he saw a skinny pale man clad only in shorts, sprawled on a needle-point wing chair. Durell looked at him and wondered what the newspapers would make of this picture of a national legislator relaxing for the week end.

A woman's high, erotic laughter bubbling with drink touched him like the rough edge of a file. It came from the terrace near the beach fence. In the yellow floodlights, he recognized her, without her typical charcoal-gray business suit, as one of the more waspish Washington gossip columnists. The man with her was a lobbyist currently being questioned by the G.O.C. subcommittee. The woman staggered through the gate to the beach and the man moved out of sight after her. In other chairs he saw a high-ranking member of State, a general's uniform, another legislator, a professional administrator of foreign aid.

He did not see Corinne.

"Come on," Hackett said impatiently.

"This isn't the place for me," Durell told him. "Not with the cops after me."

"They don't see you. They don't want to and they wouldn't dare. They wouldn't be surprised at anyone showing up here. But as long as you're with me, they won't question anything."

"How can you be sure? That Freeley woman is looking straight at me." Durell saw another columnist start to wave, then suddenly lower her hand and turn her head away as if it had been snapped by a string. "She knows who I am."

"For a minute, she knew you. Not any more."

"You're very sure of your people."

"Very."

"Quite a club," Durell said. "Who is the host?"

"Come along," Hackett said. "You'll meet him."

They went into the house through a side door. Immediately facing him on the opposite wall, Durell recognized a Rubens that had recently sold at a private sale for well over a hundred thousand dollars. There was French provincial furniture, softly glowing with centuries of hand polishing, Aubusson tapestries, Louis XV chairs, an enormous Sarouk carpet over Belgian tiles, a Greek head in marble with the nose broken off. Money had been spent here with a frantic and lavish hand, and the result was a hodgepodge where each treasure clashed and fought and died in the suffocating pressure of all the others around it.

Hackett gestured to a chair.

"Wait here, Durell." He started away, then returned. "Have you got a gun?"

"Yes."

"Perhaps you'd better give it to me."

"No. I don't trust you out of my sight," Durell said.

"I could have taken it from you. You're in no position to dictate terms, you know."

"We'll see when we come to it."

Something glimmered in the lean, clever, cruel face. "Then you do have something to bargain?"

Durell ignored the question and gestured toward the patio. "Does this go on all the time?"

"Quite often. I'll send in a drink." Hackett grinned. "Make yourself comfortable. It might not last."

He went out. Durell lit a cigarette, sat down, looked at his watch. He had seen no sign of Corinne, but he knew where the sea wall was located. He smoked for several minutes, with the feeling that unseen eyes were upon him. He heard the surf, the music, the shrill and hysterical laughter of a woman, the deeper rumbling of a man's voice.

He stood up silently, and as he turned toward the French doors, a waiter came through the doorway behind him carrying a tray with decanters and pink goblets.

"Your drink, sir?"

"Bourbon on ice," Durell said.

"Yes, sir."

Through the French doors he saw more faces he knew, prominent Washingtonians with their faces flushed, eyes heated and shining, the women shrill and anticipating the rest of the night. He found it difficult to accept.

"Bourbon on ice, sir."

He took the drink from the tall colored waiter, and on second glance decided the man was an Indian, perhaps Canadian Algonquin. "Thanks. Where is the host?"

"I couldn't say, sir."

"Don't go. Do any of these people know his name?"

"Some of them, sir. Most of them know Mr. Hackett, of course. It's the usual guest list for the week end."

"Regular affair?"

"Yes, sir."

"Who *is* the host, anyway?"

The waiter's face was dark, blank. "Mr. Hereward Quenton, sir. Will that be all?"

Durell exhaled softly. He looked at the waiter's face, saw nothing there. "I'm looking for a young lady named Miss Ybarra. A redhead. Have you seen her around?"

"On the beach, sir. But you are to wait here."

"Swimming?"

"I could not say what she is doing there, sir. She went out with the Colonel's lady. Mrs. Gibney, that is."

"Thank you."

"My name is Charles, sir."

Durell gave him a ten-dollar bill with his empty glass. "Thanks, Charles."

There was a flickering in the Indian's eyes. "Please stay here, sir. It will be best."

"Don't worry about me," Durell said.

"No, sir. I won't worry. I leave that up to Mr. Hackett."

He moved away silently with his tray of drinks.

After a moment Durell stepped out on the front patio. No one paid any attention to him. When the guests looked his way, they seemed to look right through him. He saw two men in dark suits at the gateway in the beach fence, and he turned aside and walked back down the shell drive, past the line of parked cars in the shadows. When he came to Hackett's Austin-Healey, he turned left on the road toward the high sea wall that blocked off his view of the beach. The sea wall was an extension of the cedar fence.

A flight of stone steps led to the top of the wall. He mounted swiftly, surveyed the drop to the sand below, and jumped, let his knees flex easily, and stood up in deep shadows.

To his right was the nude group around the picnic fire, but their numbers had thinned, scattered toward either the black, floodlighted surf or the rise of dunes and twisted jetties beyond. The wind was warm, and beyond the circle of the fire the moonlight made a silvery patina on the land and sea. He looked for Corinne. She was not here. The picnic fire was perhaps two hundred feet away.

He called her name, softly.

From nowhere, seemingly, a woman sprang up from the shadows of the yielding sand at the foot of the sea wall. She blocked his way. She was about forty, flat-chested, her hips bony. She was nude. Her narrow, intense face was heavily made up.

"Well, hello, there!" she shrilled. "What are you doing with all your clothes on? It's against the *rules!* You look positively *disgusting!*"

"I just got here," Durell said quietly.

"Well, hurry and *join* us! Shoo! No prudes allowed, you know! After all, we're all grown up, you know." She laughed shrilly. Her eyes were black holes in her moon-bathed face. "Hurry back. Ask for me. I'm Isabel."

"I'm looking for Corinne Ybarra," Durell told her. He did not want to look at her, but he knew that if he glanced away, she would sense his rejection and make an issue out of it. "Have you seen her?"

"She's with Mary."

"Mrs. Gibney?"

A skinny arm waved and flapped. "Down the beach. Mary followed her with blood in her eye." A giggle came from the black, stretched mouth. "You never saw such a sight. *Honestly!* Mary Gibney, *au naturel!* Really, the most disgusting specimen. And quite drunk, y'know. Oh, quite! Otherwise, she would never— You know how sensitive she is. Or must be. After all, with all those *rolls and rolls*— It's absolutely nauseating."

"Where can I find her?"

The arm flapped bonily again. "Mary is quite drunk—oh, quite—and I hope she gives that bitch of a Corinne what's coming to her. If you're smart, Mr. Ugh, you won't bother with Corinne tonight. And really, you mustn't be here on the beach like that. House rules, you know. It's such an adolescent attitude most people have, about clothing. After all, as I said, we're all *adults.* So hurry, and come back here. To me. Isabel."

"I'll try," Durell said.

The skinny woman stepped back a little. Her face became uglier. "What *is* the matter with you, anyway? Don't you *like* me?"

"Sure," Durell said. "I'll be back."

"You bastard," she hissed. "Oh, I could kill you all!"

"Have fun," Durell said.

He walked past her down the beach, beyond the fringe of lurid light from the picnic fire. There was a sour taste in his throat. At the nearest jetty, he turned in the shadows and looked back. The nude woman was staring after him, hands on her bony hips. Beyond her, hesitating on the patio entrance to the beach, were the two men in dark suits, tall and burly. There was a purposeful look to their thick necks and narrow heads as they glanced up and down the beach. Charles, the waiter, stood with them. Durell walked around the sand-blown pilings onto the next section of the beach.

The change was startling, from planned landscaping to the original, primitive wilderness untouched by bulldozer or construction engineer. The sea wind whispered and rattled in tall, reedy grasses growing over the dunes. The surf thundered. No one was in sight to the next half-buried jetty, about a hundred yards away.

He walked that way, the sand dragging at his shoes.

The picnic fire and the two guards were out of sight now, but Durell had no illusions about his time for freedom. He searched the beach and the dunes anxiously for a glimpse of the redheaded girl. She had not been at the meeting place that she herself had specified, yet her attitude on the telephone had been one of desperate urgency. Remembering the skinny woman's words, Durell felt the thin edge of anxiety cut into him, and he began to trot toward the distant jetty.

Beyond, the wilderness of sand and sea and night sky stretched in a long curve, vacant under the impassive moon. He saw nothing, no one. He wondered if the nude woman had lied to him. She was a type, Durell knew, that might derive vindictive pleasure from that petty sort of thing; and she had been more than half drunk. He paused, not sure of his next move.

That was when he heard, above the crash and thunder of the surf, a stifled, muted scream that bubbled up over the warm sea wind and then was abruptly choked off.

He halted and looked toward the surf. There had been something in the sound that prickled the skin on the nape of his neck. He saw nothing extraordinary. The black combers curled around the leaning piles of the jetty, and the jetty itself thrust obstinately into the surf while the seas burst like massive white flowers around it. The tides had scooped out dark pools here and there, and in one of the pools there was a white thrashing that for a moment he confused with the bursting combers.

He heard another brief, bubbling scream. It was weaker this time. It came from the farthest pool beside the jetty. Durell spun and ran toward the water, the sand hissing and dragging underfoot.

The surf was only knee-deep in the shadows cast by the jetty. A comber battered him, drenched him to the chest, and burst against the pilings. He saw the thrashing movement again.

White limbs, dark-red hair streaming, a blanched and terror-stricken face. Corinne. She half rose from the black water, stumbling, crying out something. A monstrous mass of white flesh surged after her. There was something elephantine and inexorable in the way the second woman overtook the floundering girl. A massive arm shot out, caught the slender form, twisted her about. Corinne went down under the surface. In the pallid moonlight, Durell saw the other woman clearly. He had never seen a truly fat woman without protective clothing before. He glimpsed the round, babyish face, dark with primitive fury, over the quaking hills and mounds of enormous breasts and buttocks. The ponderous weight settled on Corinne's struggling body and slowly and deliberately crushed the girl under the water.

chapter ELEVEN

DURELL shouted.

Either the fat woman did not hear or she was past being concerned. She was intent on murder. The push of the combers dragged at Durell's plunging progress, then the backwash pulled him forward. When he was still ten feet away, the fat woman looked up. She stared with blank, uncomprehending eyes in her baby's face. Her mouth, small and deli-

cate, strained open. Then she lifted her enormous weight, like
a white, bulbous Leviathan.

"Get away from me," she breathed.

"Let her go."

"She's dead!"

"Mrs. Gibney—"

The fat woman began to giggle, and her body shook and
trembled with the convulsive, hysterical sound. Durell pushed
past her and groped for the long, glimmering white shape of
Corinne's limp body. Her skin felt warm and smooth and wet
as he caught her thigh, then encircled her waist and lifted her
from the water. The dark-red hair streamed as her face came
up. She coughed and gagged and struggled against his grip.

"Easy, Corinne," he said.

They stood in waist-deep water. As he started to turn toward the fat woman and the shore, Mrs. Gibney swung an
arm like a monstrous ham. The blow caught him like an ax
at the back of his neck. He stumbled, dropped Corinne. An
enormous weight came thrashing after him, pushing him
down. He grabbed for the girl, caught at her, and struggled
to rise. Again that massive forearm smashed at him. He
heard the deep, vast sound of the fat woman's breathing.
Twisting, he pulled back, away from her Gargantuan blows.
He kept his grip on Corinne. A comber struck his back, pushing him toward the advancing bulbous flesh that opposed
him. There was muscle under that shuddering mountain of
pink, wet flesh. The weight against him was enormous, and
he felt smothered, panic slicing hot knives into him.

Another comber helped him break free. Corinne sagged on
one arm, her mouth open, her eyes staring in the dim moonlight. She was only partly conscious. Durell moved back toward the beach, feeling the tug of surf and the tide against
his trembling legs.

"Mrs. Gibney . . ."

The fat woman stood thigh-deep in the swirling water,
staring as if she recognized his presence for the first time.
Some of the insane, hysterical rage melted from her face. Her
tiny pink mouth opened nervously.

"Go on. Go on, take her. I'm sorry . . . sorry. . . ."

Durell carried the redheaded girl to the beach. Behind him,
advancing ponderously through the surf, came the fat woman.
He did not trust Mrs. Gibney's sudden surrender. When he
considered it safe, he lifted Corinne's slim, pale body fully in

his arms and carried her to the high, grass-grown dune above the jetty. She leaned against him when he put her down, clinging to his neck with a strength that betrayed her state of mind. There was a warm firmness to her body, the look of a dryad to her slender legs and narrow waist. He caught the glimmer of opaque white under her lids.

"Let me go, Corinne," he said quietly. "You're all right now."

"Sam?"

"Sit up," he ordered.

She coughed, gagged, pushed back her hair with a vague gesture. "I tried to meet you . . . but she followed me . . . and tried to kill me."

"All right," he said.

He forced her arms from around him and looked across the moonlit beach. From the dune he could see the picnic fire some distance away, but he did not glimpse either of the two thick-necked bouncers. The wind rattled the dry, reedy grass over his head. Then he saw Mrs. Gibney advancing toward him again. The fat woman had found two large beach towels and she had wrapped one around her massive figure. When she approached, she tossed one with contempt toward Corinne.

"Cover yourself, you nasty little whore," she said.

Corinne looked up with fear glistening on her face. "You tried to kill me," she said in wonderment.

"I'm only sorry I didn't succeed." Mrs. Gibney's face was composed now. Under the multiple layers of flesh, her bone structure seemed small and delicate. Her face could have been pert, and even beautiful, if one could ignore the glutinous fat below. Her hands were small and dimpled, her feet almost tiny. She looked at Durell. "I want to talk to you," she said bluntly. "Corinne will be all right if she's left alone for a few moments."

"Don't go, Sam," Corinne said quickly. "Don't leave me."

"Are you Mr. Durell?" Mrs. Gibney asked.

"Yes."

"Don't you know that the police are looking for you?"

"Yes."

"You don't seem very much concerned about it."

"I am. Are you going to notify them that I'm here?"

"We can talk about that." The fat woman stood waiting, watching Corinne. Durell saw that under Mrs. Gibney's sudden composure, the hysteria still quivered, like a banked fire ready to burst into flame again. He made up his mind quickly.

"Corinne, there's an Austin-Healey parked in the driveway near the sea wall. It's Hackett's. He left the key in it. Go there and get in it and wait for me."

Her ripe mouth trembled. She hugged the towel carelessly around her body. "I'm afraid to go back there."

"I'll be along as soon as Mrs. Gibney finishes. It's all right now."

She still hesitated. Her thick dark hair clung to the shape of her small head, curled wetly about her throat and shoulders. She looked at the surf and shuddered. She looked small and helpless for a moment, like a frightened, bedraggled child. Then she glanced up at Mrs. Gibney's mountainous figure and her face changed, hardened, grew vicious and mean.

"You fat slob," she whispered. "If you hadn't caught me by surprise, you couldn't have done it. You ugly pig! You bag of jelly! You—"

"That's enough," Durell said sharply. "Get going."

Corinne stood up disdainfully, facing the fat woman, whose babyish face was turned in the shadow against the moonlight. The wind whimpered in the grasses of the dune. Mrs. Gibney made an answering sound in her throat. Durell pushed the girl forward

"Go ahead. I'll see you at the car in ten minutes."

"Sam, be careful."

"I'm not worried about Mrs. Gibney."

"But they'll be looking for you. Right here."

"Do they know I was to meet you?"

"I'm not sure. I told Henry—Colonel Gibney."

"All right. Start walking."

She glanced with contempt at the fat woman once more, made a Gallic gesture of derision, and then climbed down from the grass-grown dune. Durell stood watching her free, proud stride until she had gone beyond the jetty toward the picnic fire. Nobody bothered her. He drew a deep breath and turned to Mrs. Gibney. The fat woman was looking at the moon-silvered sea. Her face quivered and shook. As he watched her, she sank ponderously to her massive knees and leaned forward, her face in her hands. The Gargantuan flesh shook and trembled as she began to sob. Durell fished in his wet pockets for a cigarette, found the pack sodden, and threw it away. His gun, in his inside coat pocket, had remained reasonably dry.

"Mrs. Gibney."

He heard her sobbed words from behind her small, dimpled hands. "I'm fat . . . fat. Ugly and horrible."

"You could probably do something about that," he said quietly, "if you wanted to."

"No, no. . . ."

"Is that why you tried to kill Corinne?"

"I don't know what happened to me. But I hate her so . . . Yes, I once looked like she does." The babyish face came up, stained with tears that were silver in the moonlight. Her eyes were beautiful, even though they were swollen by her sobbing. "Do you believe that?"

"Why not?" he asked. "But you don't go around wanting to kill every young girl you see. Why pick on Corinne?"

"Because of Henry," she whispered. Her huge shoulders slumped under the towel that covered her. "I surprised her—with Henry. I don't blame him for not wanting me, or for ignoring me that way. But I wish—I've so often hoped—"

"That's not the whole reason," Durell said.

"No. Of course not."

"What's the rest of it?"

"Roger is the rest of it. My son."

"Corinne knew him?"

"Roger wrote about her, long before he—before he was caught in East Berlin. He wrote that he'd met a wonderful French girl and wanted to marry her."

"What was he doing over the line, by the way?"

"I don't know, I don't know," she moaned.

"Why should you try to kill your son's girl, then?" he asked.

She looked up, her big childish eyes reflecting tragedy. "Don't you see? Roger's girl—he loves her—and she, with Roger's father, with her background—"

"Why should she do that?"

"Because she must be thoroughly rotten. She's vicious and evil. And she's a spy."

He waited.

"She's working for the Quenton crowd. You must not trust her, Mr. Durell. You're in very serious trouble, I understand. You're in that trouble simply because Henry is half crazy with worry, trying to keep Roger alive over there, hoping he can keep them from killing him. I know what Henry has done. And why he forced you to do what you did. And it's killing him, too. But he can't help himself. I think I would do the same, if I had the opportunity. I'm not sure. Roger is all I have. My only son. I don't want them to kill him. I'd do anything they ask, as long as they don't hurt him."

"If Corinne is Roger's girl," Durell asked, "why should she work for Quenton and try to stop you from helping Roger, all at the same time?"

"I don't know," the fat woman moaned. "She came to us a month ago and introduced herself. We took to her, at first. Henry was very fond of her. She knew Roger so well, it was almost like a visit from him." Her small hands fluttered to her face, then sank down again, as if the weight of her massive arms was too much for her. She bowed her head. "I'm so ashamed. You saw me. I'm so ugly," she said irrationally. "Nobody has ever seen me like that for—for years. Not even Henry. Especially not Henry. But I— Those people down the beach—they have a rule on nights like this. You can't go on the beach unless you—unless you go like the rest of them. It's all false, you know. All an excuse for their licentious parties. I'm not a prude, Mr. Durell. But it's shocking and disgraceful, seeing those people who hold responsible positions come here and behave the way they do. Thank goodness they're in a tiny minority in Washington. Their excuse is the strain and tensions of their jobs. But it's only an excuse, you know. They're no good. It's a small cult, almost, that Mr. Quenton has collected around him. They're all birds of a feather." She looked up at him. "You should never have come here. It's a trap for you."

"Perhaps you can help me," he suggested gently.

She nodded, chins folding over and over each other. "I've been thinking about that. You can stay with us. We're only half a mile down the beach. And although Quenton permitted only a few of us to stay here at Cramden on his sufferance, I don't think he would dare order our house searched. I'll hide you there."

"Is Corinne your house guest, too?"

She made a sound of contempt. "The police want her, too, I understand. But Henry says that Mr. Quenton ordered him to give her shelter."

"Haven't the police been around here, looking for her?"

"Oh, yes. But Mr. Quenton has this island set up legally

as a municipality, and his own men are in charge of the police. It's a farce, of course, but no one dares challenge it. The government people went off somewhere else after speaking to Mr. Quenton."

He felt cold, as if a knife had been thrust into him.

"I had no idea it was like this."

He paused. There was something here that he did not understand, that contradicted itself. It did not seem possible that the agencies looking for him would actually back down from Quenton and deny the obvious possibility that Corinne and he were hiding here. Yet Mrs. Gibney spoke as if he would be safe here. And Corinne had implied the same. He did not feel safe.

The fat woman stood up. It was a major operation, and he had to check his impulse to offer a hand, knowing she would resent it. She rolled first to one massive haunch, doubled a flabby leg the girth of a small tree, grunted, lifted herself to one knee, pushed upward with a hand on her leg, and stood, panting a little. She pushed at her pale wet hair and wrapped the beach towel more tightly around her bulging figure.

"You must think I'm an awful fool," she said quietly.

"No. You have your problems."

"You don't strike me as a man willing to sell out his country just for money," she went on. There was quick intelligence in her eyes as the moonlight washed over her babyish face. "You look like a man with much on his conscience, but not the sort that Henry might safely deal with in order to satisfy *them*."

"I owe your husband a great deal of money."

"He told me about the bridge games. But Henry is naïve."

Danger touched him in her quiet voice. "What do you mean?"

"A man like you—Henry should have troubled to inquire about your record. He's so frantic for Roger's safety that he isn't his normal self. He didn't check into your background very thoroughly."

Durell was still. "And you did?"

"You couldn't possibly have lost that much money to Henry unless you did so with deliberate intent. Henry is an abominable bridge player. And you have a record as something of an expert."

He was silent, staring at her. The wind threw spray against his cheek. He smelled the salt of the sea.

"Why does one think that fat people must necessarily be slow and stupid?" Mrs. Gibney asked gently. Her smile was quite small. "You are a dangerous man, Mr. Durell. Henry may be fooled by you, but I am not. I know that you are not what you pretend to be. Some aspects about you puzzle me—your trial today, which certainly was not a false pretense. And your escape. On the other hand, you are after something I may not want you to have."

"Such as?" he asked quietly.

"It might be Henry. I wouldn't want you to hurt him."

"I may have to," he admitted bluntly.

"Or Roger. If you do anything to jeopardize Roger's safety while he's a prisoner over there . . ." She paused.

"Yes?"

"Then I may have to kill you, Mr. Durell," she said.

chapter TWELVE

A CLOUD drifted over the face of the moon. The sea wind felt cold through Durell's wet clothing. From far down the beach, where the picnic fire still burned, came a tattered fragment of dim laughter. He looked that way and saw against the luminous sky the outline of Hackett's two guards, big and dark atop the jetty, their narrow heads and thick necks thrust forward like twin birds of prey. They were scanning the dune where he stood with Mrs. Gibney, looking directly at him.

Mrs. Gibney had not seen them. She said, "I hope you take my warning seriously, Mr. Durell."

"I know you mean it. Who are those men?"

She looked toward the high jetty. Her dimpled hand fluttered. "They work for Amos Hackett. Quenton, really. Are they looking for you?"

"I think so. But I need ten minutes with Corinne first."

"Will you hurt Roger, Mr. Durell?"

"I'll try not to."

"Tell me why you're here," she insisted. "I want to know. If I can, I might help you. You can stay with Henry and me. You can be safe there. I don't think Quenton would dare try anything violent. If only I knew—"

There was no more time. One of the men leaped lightly to the sand from the jetty, his body quick and pantherish. The other followed. They trotted at an easy gait, side by side, along the beach toward the grassy dune where he stood with the fat woman. Their advance was swift and silent and purposeful. Mrs. Gibney sucked in a slow breath.

"Will you stall them for me?" Durell asked quickly.

"Yes. Hurry. I'll meet you at my house. Corinne will show you where it is. Run!"

Durell retreated over the crest of the dune. The two men down the beach saw his move and abruptly cut away from the water's edge and ran at a diagonal to intercept him in the wild salt-water bogs inland of the dunes. Their trot became a swift loping run. Durell slid down the opposite side of the dune into knee-deep water, thrashed forward for a dozen steps, and came upon another weedy rise. The sea was out of sight. The moon was hidden behind thin clouds, but the scene was washed by warm starlight. He took the gun from his pocket and looked to right and left. House lights twinkled distantly to the north. But he wanted to go south, back of the sea wall, where Corinne waited for him. *If* she waited.

The two men suddenly appeared on the crest of the dune, rising from the earth with shocking suddenness. They looked big and dark and ominous against the night sky. Metal glinted in the hand of the first man. Then Mrs. Gibney appeared, too, calling to them. They turned their heads toward her, but they did not swing aside.

Durell backed toward the high ridge of land that formed the backbone of the island. The road was in that direction. If he could double back on the landward side and circle around the Quenton place, he might not be too late to reach Corinne. A shout followed him as he threshed through another salt-water inlet. He looked back, lifted the gun in his hand. The two men came on fast, along a dry path they knew, cutting down the distance with alarming speed. Durell spun north, running through high wild grass. He looked back again and saw only one of his pursuers. The other had vanished. He twisted left toward the road, saw the distant power poles stark against the night sky. Then the second man suddenly appeared, directly ahead of him.

Durell ran straight for him.

The second man stopped in surprise. He had a gun in his hand, but it was lowered, muzzle pointing to the sand. His face was a narrow wedge of white in the moonlight. His mouth opened like a dark slit and the gun started up as Durell dived at him from the top of the dune. A strangled shout ripped the night air. Then Durell slammed into him and the other stumbled and clawed backward, lost his footing, and twisted on one hand and knee, struggling to rise. Durell chopped at him with his gun and the man rolled down the dune ahead of him. Durell jumped, landed with both knees on the man's chest, and hit him again. There was a fury in him that lifted his arm once more, a rage like a wild storm shaking him. He checked the last blow. It was unnecessary. The man was out, a burly clod of flesh no longer dangerous to him. He rose and ran for the highway.

There was no more pursuit. Beyond the road was a hedge of wild chokecherry, low and scrubby, and he followed the line of sheltering brush until he was safely beyond the lights of the Quenton house before he doubled back toward the sea. The party was still going on, quieter now, and as he approached the sea wall he saw that the picnic fire was only a glowing heap of dying ashes.

The Austin-Healey was still where Hackett had left it, at the end of the driveway close to the sea wall. He approached it with caution, looking for signs of renewed chase from the big house nearby. He saw no one. The two men who had pursued him had not returned.

The English sports car seemed empty.

Then as he opened the door he saw Corinne's figure loom up from where she had been crouching. Her arms snaked out, white and firm and still cold-wet, and she pulled him toward her awkwardly.

"I thought you would never get here," she breathed. "Oh, be quick. I'm sick. Hurry, Sam."

The keys were still in Hackett's car. Durell slid onto the low leather seat beside the girl. Corinne was careless with the beach towel. He saw in the moonlight the firmness of one breast, the smooth curve of hip and thigh. She seemed unaware of herself. He heard her teeth chatter.

"Take it easy," he said.

"Just get me away from here. Please—hurry."

He started the motor, backed quickly down the shell drive,

turned hard, and drove to the wide sand road that led away from the house. He did not turn on the headlights.

"Go left," Corinne said.

"But that's the end of the island."

"You cannot go the other way. They have guards. Didn't you see them?" She huddled close to him, her face dim and vague inside the car. "We have only a little time before they catch us. It is certain to happen."

"You've been here before, then."

"Yes. Many times. I have walked around. I know the island well."

He turned left. The road promptly deteriorated into dim twin ruts, and he guided himself by the wash of pale moonlight. The house was quickly lost behind a line of wild dunes.

He did not drive fast. The island narrowed rapidly until he could see the wide, black reach of the ocean on both sides, laced with white combers over the shallows and bars. The wheels splashed hard as he forded a tidal creek. Corinne's teeth kept chattering. Her hands touched him, resting on his arm and thigh, as if to assure herself that he was there.

"Behind that jetty," she said finally. "Hardly anyone ever comes here."

"Is anyone waiting?" he asked bitterly.

"Why should anyone wait here for us?"

"You arranged for Hackett and his men to follow me the last time you directed me for a drive."

"Oh, please. Trust me. I had to do it."

He turned the English car out of the ruts into deep, black shadow cast by crooked pilings. The jetty was ancient and barnacled, partially buried in the eternally shifting sands. The surf was much rougher here than at the house. Its thunder filled the air and shook the earth. The wind felt colder, too, blowing from the empty east. There was a primitive loneliness to this spot that touched a sympathetic chord in him, reminding him of places in the bayous that seemed so ancient and primeval that it was almost sacrilegious to enter.

He cut the motor and sat still.

Corinne shivered and crept close to him on the car seat. Her long legs pressed against him.

"I feel as if I am flying apart. You know?" she whispered. He saw the smooth muscles of her jaw twitch as she fought to keep her teeth from chattering again. "I feel as if there is something in my head about to burst. I am going to be sick."

"Go ahead. Then we'll talk."

"Do not be cruel, Sam!"

"I owe you nothing," he pointed out.

"But we are both in desperate trouble. We are lost. Why can't we be friends? Allies?"

"I could name a few reasons."

"I will tell you anything you want to know. I can help you. We can help each other. Perhaps we can run away from it, get out of the country. It's what *they* will offer you —but you mustn't accept their help. You and I could find some place where nobody would know us, where they won't catch us. Couldn't we do that?"

"No." He spoke from experience and knowledge. "There's no place under the sun or sky or on land, no place at all, Corinne, that would be safe for us. Not for people like you and me. Not for people who have done what we've done."

She drew a little away from him, chilled, and hugged the towel around her as if suddenly aware of herself. She stared at the sea. He saw the silver shine of tears on her face. Her hair looked black in the moonlit pattern of light and shadow in the car. She bent forward and covered her face with her slim hands and wept silently.

He let her weep. He did not touch her. He did not comfort her.

There was loneliness in this small shadowed area of sand and sea. Danger lived in him and beside him, yet he felt detached and safe. How much time did he have? They were looking for him now. They would miss Hackett's car, check the guards, and eventually come this way. There was no escape. He did not want escape. All he wanted was a little time. A little of the truth.

Corinne rubbed her eyes with a child's gesture. "I'm sorry. You are very patient with me."

"You know why."

"You want the papers you lost?"

"Where are they?"

"I don't have them, Sam. I never had them."

"This is not the time for lying," he said.

"I do not lie. I know how to lie; I admit that. I am not a very nice person. I have tried to be, since coming to this country, but they would not let me. But to you I want to be fine and good, and I won't lie, Sam. After you took the envelope back from me last night, I never saw it again."

"Hackett says he doesn't have it."

"I don't understand."

"The only reason they brought me here and are hunting for me right now—and maybe they want to kill me now—is because Hackett wants that file. I don't have it. They don't have it. So it must be you."

"No," she whispered. "Please believe me!"

Anger surged in him. He wanted to slap the truth from her. He did not trust her. He turned, then, and looked at the thunderous surf, the glimmering line of the beach. The moon was low in the west. The night was darker, cooler. The wind was thinly edged, blowing from the wild Atlantic. He fought with his anger and looked down at the girl and saw her face lifted in appeal.

"Why did you telephone to me?" he asked.

"I wanted to do something decent and help you, Sam. They want you, of course. They can offer you safety. Maybe even a trip abroad, to Europe, where you can lose yourself. I wanted to warn you not to trust them."

"Are you talking about Quenton?"

She nodded mutely.

"You work for him?"

Another nod. She said, "It is a long story. Please sit down. Here, beside me. It is not pleasant to talk about. I never told anyone. But they found out about me and they will tell Colonel Gibney—Roger's father—and they will see to it that Roger knows, too. Then my life will be over. I am tired of fighting like an animal for a little quiet time in which to live. Very tired. So I did what they asked of me."

She spoke without looking at him. Her voice was flattened, a monotone without the inflection of emotion. He sat on the sand beside her. Salt spray stung his face. She hugged the towel around her and stared at the ocean.

"Sometimes I think I should have died long ago," she said. "Why do we struggle so hard to live? Why do we search so long for love? There was a time when I would have laughed at these questions, long ago, during the war. I was only fourteen, but I knew all about men, everything. I wanted life, and they wanted me, and I exchanged myself for what they could give me. Those were the Vichy days.

I had no politics. It was not a question of being a patriot with the *Maquis* and learning enemy secrets while I was in bed with them. Life was quite elemental, actually. One fought and schemed for bread, for nylons, for cigarettes. And perhaps a kind word, even though it was spoken in German with a hidden sneer. I did not care. I lived through it."

Durell said, "You don't have to tell me this."

"I want you to understand what I am, that is all."

"I think I do."

"Later, after the war, I was driven out. I went to Barcelona. I was a singer." Pride edged her voice for a moment. "Once I had an engagement for two weeks in La Floridita, in Madrid. It was wonderful. I earned a good salary. I was respectable. Then people who knew me from Vichy days in Marseilles saw me and I was fired and a Spanish gentleman was kind to me and helped me. Then I met Roger Gibney."

"In Spain?"

"He was working at the Air Force fields there. He was in Madrid on a holiday. There was something about him—something wonderful. Can you understand? I cannot explain it."

"You fell in love."

Her laughter was harsh. "Yes, imagine it! How ridiculous! I fell in love."

"Not ridiculous."

She looked down at the sand and whispered, "For me it was something wonderful and frightening and tragic."

"Did you tell him about yourself?"

"A little of it. But I was too afraid."

"Did he understand?"

"I think so. He was wonderful to me. I followed him to Berlin when he was transferred there."

"And your Spanish gentleman?"

"I left him the day I met Roger." She shivered. "It is a dreary tale, is it not? An ugly history. Nothing that a respectable family like the Gibneys could accept."

"They don't know about it?"

"I hope not. When Roger was captured in East Berlin, I came over here. I could stand Europe no longer. I wanted to meet his parents and tell them Roger and I were in love, to comfort them and wait with them for his release. I found Sidonie, my cousin. She helped me get the job in K Section as a translator. I speak many West European languages. I should," she said bitterly. "I was intimate with many of them."

"But you also worked for the Q people," he said.

"Yes. It was not long before Amos Hackett came to me. He took me to lunch and recited my history, every ugly page of it. It is amazing how much he knew. There were even some things I had forgotten. And he asked how it would go with me if the Gibneys learned all of that."

"Blackmail?"

"I understood his kind of man at once. I knew there could be no pity in him. So I belonged to him, and my soul was no longer mine again."

"He made you spy for Q?"

"He wanted information. Most of it seemed unimportant. And he paid me. He paid me well."

"You gave him classified information?"

"There are many others working for him like me."

"Girls, being blackmailed?"

"And men."

"They must have an extensive filing system of data on all of their employees, then."

"Yes, they have."

"Do you know where it's kept?"

She shook her head. Her dark hair swung across her face. She leaned forward with her arms on her knees, and the moonlight made her exposed back look satin-smooth and warm.

"I have looked," she said. "They have photographs, affidavits, all sorts of things to prove what they know. I hoped I might find it somewhere and destroy it, and then be free again. But I will never find it. And I will never be free." Suddenly she turned to him, the towel sliding to the dark sand between them. Her face was anguished, her voice a whimper. "Oh, Sam—help me, help me!"

She came against him like a burrowing animal, her silken body shaking. Her teeth chattered again. He put his arm around her, pity moving him, and she flung herself against him in an agony that produced great wrenching movements of her arms and legs.

"Love me," she gasped. "I almost died tonight. I want to know that I'm still alive! I want to live. Love me!"

She moved against him in great, warm waves of twisting desire. He heard her quick, gasping breath as her hands sought him searchingly. The moon was only a dim glimmer on the landward horizon. His feeling of isolation expanded until the cool sand was like an impervious stronghold protecting them from the moment when disaster might threaten again. He did not know how long they would be safe. For the moment he did not care.

"Corinne . . ."

She was sinuous, quick, adept. The soft curves of her body gleamed and undulated, now above him, now beside him, now beneath him. Her eyes were wide, staring up at the deep vault of the starry sky. The sound of the surf grew thunderous in his ears until it filled the universe. Her arms encompassed him in a tight, frantic grip.

"Roger, darling," she moaned. "Oh, Roger!"

Gasping, she spent herself and was suddenly very still beside him, her long legs flexed, her head arched back, her tumultuous breathing slowed. He drew away from her and sat up.

Corinne reached for the towel and wrapped herself carefully in it, sitting beside him. The beach on either hand was still deserted. She looked at the sea for a long moment.

"So you still love Roger," Durell said.

"I am sorry. Yes."

"Don't apologize for it. I'm glad."

"Are you? Thank you for pretending to be him."

He looked up and down the beach again. The cool wind had freshened. The grassy dunes moved, shifting in the uncertain light. Shadows swayed here and there. He wondered if they had been watched.

"Then you work for Quenton's spy organization just to help Roger," he said. "Is that it?"

"Q isn't a spy outfit," she said.

"Then what is it?"

"I don't know. I don't understand it." She drew a deep breath. Her face was calm now, quiet and lovely in the dim starlight. She stared at the silver sea. "Quenton is not a traitor. The old man may seem to help those who are, but the face he presents to the public is the true one. Have you ever met him?"

"No."

"He is a fanatically loyal American. He wants this country to be supreme. He is sincere about it. Believe me, I have met demagogues and men who live and breathe only for their political beliefs. Quenton is one of them."

"But he seems ready to help me, a confessed traitor."

"I don't understand his reasons. Just as he helps Gibney."

"Who is the enemy contact with Gibney? Isn't it Quenton?"

"No. I don't think so."

"Then who is putting pressure on Gibney?"

"Quenton," she said.

"You're contradicting yourself."

"And you ask strange questions for one in your position." She looked at him and her face had changed and there was a deep question in her wide eyes. She touched his face very gently, and then he felt the faint sting of her nails drawn across his cheek, like a warning. "Are you really a traitor, Sam? Did you really steal that information they want?"

"I'm here because I was half promised a chance to get out of the country," he said.

"I wonder."

He looked over his shoulder at the sound of sand suddenly sliding and hissing down the dune behind them in a miniature avalanche. A man stood there, looking at them.

"We have company," Durell said.

It was Hackett.

chapter THIRTEEN

HE DID NOT RUN. There was no place to go, and he did not want to run any more. He helped Corinne up, and the girl shrank beside him, watching Hackett climb down the dune. Her face was pale. Other men appeared on the beach, on the dune, on the jetty. All around them.

"Durell!"

He stood still. He did not reach for his gun.

"Sam, be careful," Corinne whispered.

Hackett's face was dark with fury as he strode up to them. Two men with rifles stood straddle-legged on the dune, covering him. Durell said, "Tell your trigger men to relax, Amos. I won't shoot back."

"Give me your gun," Hackett snapped.

Durell took the gun carefully from his pocket and handed it to Hackett. Hackett smiled twistedly. He weighed the gun for a moment and without warning hit Durell in the face with it. Durell went down and heard Corinne's scream and then heard her smothered yelp of pain as Hackett slapped her aside. He was on his feet, rising, when Hackett kicked him. He went down again. Anger struggled against a cold knowledge that resistance would be suicide. Hackett wanted him to fight back, to furnish an excuse to kill him. He rolled with the blows that followed, protecting himself when he could. A burly man dragged Corinne aside and flung her to the beach. Her towel was lost in the sand. Another man hauled Durell up, twisted an arm cruelly behind his back, and pushed him toward Hackett.

"He's not so tough," said the burly man.

"Don't let him fool you," Hackett grated. He leaned forward and stared at Durell. Durell felt blood trickle down his cheek from a cut under his eye. "What kind of game do you think you're playing with us?"

"No game," Durell said.

"I told you to wait in the house."

"I wanted to talk to Corinne."

"What about?"

"The file."

"She doesn't have it." Hackett was contemptuous. "You cooked your goose, man."

Durell's face ached. He tasted blood in a corner of his mouth. A car came churning over the soft sand, and the headlights were momentarily garish on Corinne's nudity as Hackett's men flung her inside. Durell stood up. His breathing was light and easy. In the starlight, he saw Hackett looking at him with satisfaction. The man was balanced on his toes.

"Come on, Durell," Hackett said coaxingly. "You had your fun. Now give me a little trouble."

"What do you want?"

"I'm going to kill you. Something I wanted to do the first time I saw you."

There was an ugly, jumpy, jittery anticipation in Hackett. His eyes flickered darkly. Durell wiped at the blood on his mouth with a forefinger. It could happen like this, he thought, on a lonely beach, under an empty sky, after a travesty of love. He looked at the men around him. They were stamped with death. There was silence from the car where they had taken Corinne.

"Come on," Hackett said again. "You want it here, now?"

Durell stood waiting.

Hackett grinned. "That would be too easy."

There was movement to Durell's right, a quick nod from Hackett, and one of the guards hit Durell across the back with the barrel of his rifle. He throttled a scream between his teeth. Hate gorged him; he choked it down. Sand scraped the side of his face. Someone kicked him. The stars jolted from their courses, reeling. Hackett leaned over him.

"Where is it, Durell? Where are those papers?"

Durell leaped at him. . . .

Corinne was screaming.

Durell lay in darkness, and her screams came in short bursts of agony, filling every pocket of silence, every bleak corner of his mind. He floated on a sea of pain. The girl's screams became a bubbling flood of invective, broken and breathless. Another scream, and quick, abrupt silence came.

The darkness lay without and within. The room where they had taken him was small, and he did not remember too clearly the transition from beach to house. But he knew that this was Quenton's place, and he was still on the island, and it was almost dawn. When he twisted his head, straining against the bonds that tied him, he saw the dim gray rectangle of an open window, and through the window came the muted hiss and crash of the surf and the forlorn cry of a gull. He was aware of all this with a part of his mind still detached from the pain Hackett had inflicted on him.

The door opened, closed. He did not turn to look at Hackett.

"The girl passed out again," Hackett said. "She's tough. You like what we're doing to her, Durell?"

He did not answer.

"You want us to keep on with it?"

"You'll kill her."

"Oh, no. But she won't ever be pretty again. You wouldn't want her again."

Durell said nothing.

"It's up to you, Durell."

"No."

"Give us the file, that's all."

"No."

"There's a plane coming at two o'clock this afternoon. A private amphibian. From here it flies to Andros Island, in the Bahamas. A Greek gentleman there is ready to put you onto the next leg. Then the Balkans. You'll be all right over there. Safe, with no more problems."

"To hell with you."

"Give me the file. Talk to me, Durell."

"I'll talk to Quenton."

"No."

"Quenton or nobody," Durell said.

"You'll talk to me, you stubborn Cajun bastard."

Pain.

Laughter, hissing in the dawn gloom.

You let the laughter come, breaking over you like a storm at sea, and then you welcome the dark silence that follows.

Daylight brightened the room.

He thought of escape. But he did not want to escape. Where would he go? This was where he wanted to be. This was where the answer could be found.

But they'll kill you, he thought.

Not yet, he thought.

It grew hot in the room as the sunlight struck into it. He was left alone for a long time. He did not hear Corinne screaming any more. He wanted to stop what they were doing to her, but he could not help her. Maybe she was dead. He considered this, and he considered that he, too, was going to die, if he was wrong. Hackett was clear about that. He concentrated on Hackett, on hatred, on a lust in him to meet Hackett again in another time, another place. The hatred gave him strength. He studied his surroundings.

A small room, a small window, a solid paneled door. Cars came and went somewhere outside. He wondered about last night's guests. Had any of them heard Corinne screaming? And where was Quenton? He hadn't yet seen the man behind this voluptuous wealth and deliberate depravity.

The answers he wanted were somewhere, if he could hold on.

Hackett came in. He wore a singlet and slacks, and his arms were tough and wiry.

"Well, Durell?"

"Where is Quenton?"

"He'll see you when you talk."

"Does he know I'm here?"

A grin. "Possibly."

"And does he know what you're doing?"

"Maybe."

"Is the girl dead?"

"She's only stubborn."

Durell said, "I'm going to kill you, Hackett."

They looked long at each other. Hackett started to laugh, then the sound faded. There was a momentary glimmer of uncertainty in his dark eyes. A bafflement, a struggle to understand. He looked away.

"The file, Durell?"

"Let me talk to Quenton."

"You don't talk to anyone but me. You don't eat, sleep, or drink until you talk. Understand?"

"Why is it so important?" Durell asked.

Hackett pulled a chair from the wall and sat down. "It's not the file any more. It's you. Who are you, what you are. You're not in pattern, Durell. You came here looking for something. What is it? Dope on Quenton, or me? You're tagged as a rat, a traitor; but I'm beginning to wonder. I've offered you a deal, a free trip to Europe, a hop, skip, and jump over the Curtain to your friends. But you won't dicker. You won't trade. So what do you want? I could turn you over to the federal cops, and they want you bad, believe me. But maybe it's all a phony set-up. I want to know what you're after. I know the facts, all that's on the surface. And on the basis of those facts, you ought to jump at any deal we offer you. Why don't you jump, Durell?"

"Maybe your price isn't high enough."

"What more do you want?"

"A talk with Quenton."

"That's not possible."

"You can make it possible. Are you afraid of it, Hackett? Can't you admit failure? Quenton thinks of you as his good right hand, the man who never makes mistakes. And you can't afford to make mistakes, because if you do, you're out. You're dead."

"I like what I've got here, " Hackett admitted. "I like what I'm going to get."

"Do I threaten any of that?"

"You puzzle me."

"Let me talk to Quenton," Durell said.

It was dark again.

It was silent.

He stared into the darkness and listened to the silence. Somewhere across the wide sea, in a strange city in a strange land, a man known only as Antonio waited to kill, waited with death in his heart, because his woman had been taken from him. One death, the death of a nervous man—and who knew where the ripples would end? Humanity walked on a tightrope these days, balanced precariously between doom and hope. The death of one man in power could create a breeze, a little wind, that might upset humanity's balance and plunge all mankind into a pit of savagery. Who could know and who could say what might happen, if this were done or not done? There was evil around him, and treachery like a cancerous growth dimly seen through darkness. He saw a pattern, still formless and still indistinct, ahead of him down the path of treachery and deceit he had chosen to tread.

Alone in the darkness, Durell weighed success against failure, his gains against his mistakes. Hackett suspected him. Hackett sensed in him a flawed image other than the one he had hoped to present. It could not be helped. He had played a part and gained this doorway, but Corinne had also led him down other ways, and because of this, Hackett was close to learning the truth about him.

But what did Hackett want? The file. And where was it? Durell did not have it. Corinne did not have it. Certainly not the Gibneys. Who, then? If not Hackett, who?

He did not know.

Excitement suddenly grew in him. An answer was here, before him. He reached for it, grabbed at nothing, held emptiness in his hands and stared at it blankly.

Where was the file?

Who had it?

No one had it.

His mind lunged at the thought, checked, went at it again. Hackett could not admit failure. Failure meant destruction, abandonment by Quenton, who tolerated only success. Yet Durell had assumed Hackett had the file and was playing a game for private, obscure purposes. But the truth might be astonishingly simple.

No one had the file.

His mind jumped back to the first night, when he had lost it. Careful, now. Hackett and his two thugs had sprung the trap Corinne had led him into. He held no resentment against Corinne for this now. Forget Corinne. Later, Hackett had returned with Jones, the M.I. man. Why? Why, if he had already got the file in the first attempt?

Hackett didn't have it. Corinne didn't have it.

Durell lay still, pain forgotten, darkness pushed aside.

He remembered his awakening beside the dark stream, his torn pocket, his torn clothes. *The torn pocket.* And falling down that dark, scrubby slope of the ravine, landing at the bottom beside the chuckling creek. A torn pocket, a missing envelope that made the difference between honor and disgrace, between life and death.

His laughter was utterly silent, without mirth.

And Hackett came in again.

chapter FOURTEEN

HE LOOKED AT HACKETT differently and Hackett saw the difference and said, "What is it?"

"Tell me the time," Durell said.

"After ten. Why?"

"Does it look like rain?"

Hackett's thin face was puzzled. "Don't give me that. Your brain isn't addled." He jerked his head and a man came into the room with a knife that glimmered in the faint light of a lamp outside. Durell's nerves tightened. The man came over to the couch where he was tied and sliced quickly and efficiently through Durell's bonds.

"Can you stand up?" Hackett asked.

Durell tried. Hot needles plunged in and out of his

arms and legs. The pain made him sweat. He clung to the couch, straightened, took a step, went down on one knee, straightened again. He stood swaying, drawing in deep breaths of air. He could not hear the surf outside the window of the little room. Hackett signaled to his helper again and the man took a glass of water and handed it to Durell. Durell rinsed his puffy mouth, spat on the floor, rinsed again, drank some, fought against the gritty thirst in his throat. The floor heaved under him, then slowly steadied. He looked at Hackett.

"How come?"

"Quenton thinks you may have the wrong idea about us. Maybe that's what makes you so goddamn stubborn."

"All right. Let's go."

Nobody offered to help. Walking was agony for the first few steps. Hackett led the way. The guard followed. They went down a long corridor into a sun room that was all glass on three sides, facing the sea, with a fieldstone wall on the fourth side enclosing an enormous stone fireplace. Over the fireplace was a huge pair of polished steer's horns, mounted above two crossed Mexican rifles ornately inlaid with silver. A heavily carved mahogany table was set with food and crystal decanters of wine. There was a flag of Texas, ripped and battled-stained, over a gun case to the left of the fireplace. It was a robust room, a man's room, strong and comfortable.

A high, thin voice said, "Come in, come in! So this is Durell?"

"Here he is," Hackett said.

A whip cracked and tapped against a polished leather boot. One long, skinny leg crossed another, straightened, flexed. The whip snapped against leather again. Durell looked at Hereward Quenton.

A small round head, face wrinkled and seamed like leather left out in the sun and wind too long. A halo of white hair above a pinched brow that looked as if it had been squeezed into permanent furrows at birth. A petty mouth, a beak of a nose that shone white against the sunken cheeks, and watery eyes of so light a blue as to seem almost all white. Around the skinny, bony hips sagged a gun belt and a holstered, pearl-handled .44 Frontiersman that looked much too heavy for the clawlike hands to lift. There was a smell of old age in the room that neither the sea nor the polish of expensive furniture could dispel.

The watery eyes squinted. Teeth clicked loosely. "What happened to you, Durell?"

"I've been beaten, punched, kicked. You name it, Hackett did it."

"Amos, I told you those methods were entirely unnecessary!"

"He's stubborn, Senator."

"You mean he is intelligent. An intelligent man who is also a strong man cannot be handled like a thug. You're a fool, Amos."

"Yes, sir."

"Sit down, Durell."

"I'd rather stand."

"You want some medical attention?"

"No, thanks."

"Food? Did Amos starve you, too?"

"It can wait."

The little man was no more than five feet tall. He looked ludicrous with the gun belt sagging from his skinny, skeletal hips. But Durell was not amused. He did not like the look in Quenton's eyes. They were eyes accustomed to watch men jump in obedience, pettish and querulous senile eyes that had seen too much and yet lusted to see more, hugging sensation and life as a miser hoards gold. Long ago, Durell had seen eyes like that in the faces of war criminals he had hunted down in the ruins of Cologne with Lew Osbourn. Spurs jingled as Quenton walked to the tall windows and faced the dark sea.

"Our difficulty seems to be that Hackett kept you in the dark about us," Quenton said. "Amos does not like reason. He prefers force, which has its advantages and is necessary in most instances. But he does not understand a man like you, Durell. I do, you see. I must apologize for the treatment you received in my house."

Durell laughed. His face hurt. "Were you just too squeamish to watch, Senator?"

Quenton's false teeth glistened evenly. "I've seen things that would make you sick for days, young feller. I've done things you'd puke over. It's always been my rule that when matters come to a fight, there just ain't no rules. You gouge out eyes, you castrate your enemies, you kill 'em sure, and then there's nothing left to trouble you. You were treated pretty good. Amos doesn't know the fine points of askin' a man questions. There were Indians in my day, Apaches who raided in East Texas. There were no rules. I killed 'em off whenever I caught a band of 'em—braves, squaws, infants down to babes in arms. So there weren't any left."

"And that's the way you've survived since?" Durell asked.

"The rules haven't changed. Only their application. But not the kill-or-be-killed rule."

"I'm glad they ran you out of Washington at the last election, Senator."

"I don't take offense. Because, you see, I'm back, my boy."

"Not for long, I'm sure."

A cackle came from the dry, wrinkled mouth. Quenton's clawlike hand whipped with incredible speed, freeing his .44 from its holster, leveling it at Durell. The muzzle looked black and deadly, pointed between Durell's eyes.

"Who would miss you, boy, if I killed you now?"

"Probably no one."

"Then you're knocking on death's door."

"Go ahead," Durell said. "Shoot."

Quenton cackled. "By God. By God, no wonder Amos didn't get nowhere with you. I like you, boy."

"I think you stink," Durell said. "You're a rotten, sadistic, treacherous snake of an old man."

Quenton's skinny finger squeezed the trigger. The shot was thunderous in the big room. Durell felt a thunderclap in his right ear. He knew he had jerked his head instinctively to the side, and he saw the pleased reaction on the wizened old face. The bullet had chunked into the paneling over the fire-place. Durell rubbed his ear where he felt a burning sensation. His fingertip was lightly smeared with blood.

"Be careful how you talk next time," Quenton said.

"I retract nothing."

"Sit down, boy. I think we can come to terms. You hate my guts, but you don't know what I'm after and what I'm going to get. Amos, give the man a sandwich. He must be hungry. And give him some of that there special bourbon. It's fine stuff. One of the few things they make in this fancy, ladylike state is good bourbon."

"I haven't anything to sell you," Durell said. "Nothing you can bargain for."

"Yes, you have, boy. You can sell yourself. You're going to belong to me or you're going to die. It's simple, hey? If I killed you now, I'd be a hero in the nation's press tomorrow morning. I might have to kill you anyway, since Amos kept you here and made me an accomplice in aiding a fugitive from federal justice. That's a serious thing. It could do me some hurt. Hackett is going to pay for that mistake, too."

"Senator—"

"Shut up and listen. Now, Durell, tell me what you think of me—and don't waste time cussin' me out because you got a few aches and pains. Why do you think I brought you here when you busted away from that loyalty board yesterday? You think this place is a nest of spies? You think I'm the ringleader in a nasty sedition plot, is that it?"

"Perhaps."

"But there ain't a man loves this country more than me. There ain't a man tryin' harder and spending more money to keep it safe and strong, to make it the greatest, most wonderful empire God graced this old world with. America is God's gift to a sick and hungry planet, and the devil himself can't keep us from ruling them atheistic savages on the other side. Maybe we got to play ball and talk polite to the nigras and dagoes and Chinks over in Africa and Asia. But not for long. We're too strong, boy. Stronger than they know! We can lick anybody. We can take 'em all on and show 'em what we can do. And that's what we're going to do, too! Bomb 'em off the face of the earth! Wipe 'em out, clean things up, once and for all."

"Like the Indian bands long ago? Men, women, babes in arms?"

"They ain't people. They're savages. They're inferior." Quenton thrust his round head forward on his pipestem neck. "You ain't full of that idealistic crap about the equality of the human races, are you, boy? You got more sense than that. Any fool knows a white American is worth ten foreigners, any time. Seems to me we've taken enough of their lip and talked too soft to 'em for too long. Use the bombs, I say. Wipe 'em out. Make the world clean and safe for democracy."

"Texas style?" Durell asked softly.

"I don't like your tone, boy. I mean that."

"I think you're crazy. Do you *want* an atomic war?"

"It's the only answer to all our troubles."

"And you think America would win?"

"Hell, we couldn't miss. We've never been licked yet."

"But a lot of people would get killed."

"Hell, there'll just be that much more room for those left."

"I mean American people. In American cities."

"A lot of foreigners live in our cities. It'll be a good laxative for this country, boy, if some of these cities get wiped out, too."

Durell looked sidewise at Hackett. There was nothing he could read in the other's dark face. He felt incredulous. There was a ring of fanatic fervor in the old man's words. He believed what he was saying. He was fighting to bring about a holocaust that he honestly felt to be desirable. Something moved in the back of Durell's mind, a memory of words that Dickinson McFee had once spoken. It was as if some missing part of a puzzle had suddenly clicked into place, and a pattern leaped in bloody, dangerous outline into full focus. There were gaps here and there, as if the design were still incomplete. But there was enough to lift excitement in him, enough to make him forget the ugly hours behind him.

"I'm beginning to understand," Durell said slowly.

"Then can you guess why you're here?"

"I think so."

"You're a criminal. You're a curse to our nation. You were willing to sell our secrets for a handful of gold. Could I buy you back?"

"Maybe. But you don't want to," Durell said.

The watery old eyes glistened with reptilian delight. "Yep. Yep. I think you got it. You're intelligent, which Amos didn't understand. You know what I'm after. You're tough, and you've made mistakes, and you betrayed this country, but I ain't one to hold a man's mistakes against him forever, specially when he's willing to help me get what *I* want. You know what I want, don't you? You know it now?"

"Yes," Durell said quietly. "You want war."

The room was silent. The old man holstered his pearl-handled gun. Durell sat down. Hackett stood like a slat of darkness beside the door. There was no other sound from anywhere in the big, rambling house. Inside the room, a rococo clock ticked busily. It was just ten. A tiny golden bell chimed the hour.

"You're looking for an international incident," Durell said.

"We've got to be in the right, boy. We've got to make it look as if they started it."

"You know about Antonio, that Rumanian in Budapest?"

"That's his code name. Yep."

"And you know he's bent on assassination?"

Quenton chuckled. "Let's hope he makes it."

"And if they learn that Antonio is—or was—on our payroll, then the war you want might begin."

"Right."

"So you want the file I took from K Section that identifies him."

"Right."

"You'll help me evade the law and my punishment for treason if I get it for you?"

"We can make a deal. You want money, I've got money for you. You want a safe place to hide, I can put you there. Maybe you plan to sell them people your stuff, anyhow. That's why you took it, I reckon. But I can't count on you doing the job right. It will be better if my outfit handles it. Seems fair enough to me."

"You've done this before," Durell said. "In the name of your conception of patriotism."

"It's the only true patriotism, boy. We're through talking about it. We're down to business now. You got the file with that man's real name on it. I want it. You're going to give it to me."

"And if I don't?"

Quenton grinned. There was something wrong about his pale eyes, in the death's-head grimace of his weathered face. Something did not ring quite true. This old man, with his zeal and fanaticism, with the money of a Croesus to enforce his demands, had recited his aims with a certain glibness, as if the words were memorized, implanted in him from other sources. Durell shot a glance at Amos Hackett. The tall man stood with his face narrow against the lamplight. Nothing to be read there. Was it Hackett's brain and Hackett's words echoing in that toothless, childish old mouth? Durell wondered. If not Hackett, then who?

He did not know. He could not guess.

"Well, now," Quenton said with satisfaction. "Now we come right down to the nut in this palaver, Durell. You know what I want. More important, you know why I want it. You've set your price by now?"

"Yes."

"Well, then, name it."

"Where is the girl?" he asked. "Where is Corinne?"

Quenton looked at Hackett. The thin man stirred. "Asleep."

"I want to see that she's alive, for myself," Durell insisted.

"Is that your first condition?" Quenton asked.

"Yes."

"Is she alive, Amos?"

"Her face," Hackett said thinly. "I thought she was just being stubborn, like Durell. I thought if I threatened her, if I damaged her looks just a little—"

"Amos, you're a fool!"

"I did what I thought was best."

"But she's alive?"

"She'll live."

Quenton swung to Durell. "What else do you want?"

"I want Hackett," Durell said.

"Hey?"

"I want to see him dead."

Hackett laughed, then stopped laughing and cursed very softly. "You see, Senator, what I've been up against."

The reptilian, milky eyes glistened. "Very unusual, Durell."

"Hackett is no good to you any more," Durell said. "He and I won't ever work together. He's a fool in many ways. You said so yourself. We could have come to terms last night, if he hadn't been so anxious to practice his sadism on me and the girl. You couldn't trust him not to make worse mistakes."

"Shut up," Hackett whispered.

"You might be right," Quenton said and giggled.

The big .44 Frontiersman was in his hand again.

He pointed it at Amos Hackett.

Someone began to shout and scream in another part of the house.

chapter FIFTEEN

QUENTON LOWERED his gun. His jaw sagged, his teeth clicked, his pale eyes jerked from Hackett to Durell. "Go see what that was, Amos."

Hackett did not move. His thin face was sallow. A muscle twitched and jumped in his bony cheek. His eyes were dull.

"Go look for yourself. I've just quit."

"Goddamn you for an idiot!" the old man screamed. "Who did that yelling? Go and see!"

"No more orders from a crap-headed old bastard who'd sell me down the river," Hackett said thickly. "I'm through with you and your crackpot schemes."

"You can't quit!" Quenton said.

Distantly, from the other part of the house, came muted shouts and yells and a long, ululating scream. Quenton began to shiver. His skinny frame came clawing around the desk. He waggled the gun at Hackett.

"Durell, you wanted to see Amos dead?"

"Not your way," Durell said. "I want to do it."

Hackett cursed, staring at the big gun the old man held.

"Do you side with me, Durell?" the old man rasped.

"For now, yes."

"I've got to trust you. Amos, sit down. We'll talk this over—unless you go see who's making that confounded noise and why."

"No," Hackett said. "I'm through."

A grim spark of admiration for the thin man touched Durell. He knew that Quenton just might squeeze the trigger and shoot Hackett in the face. Hackett knew this, too. But he stood his ground. Durell pulled open the door. His legs trembled. Nausea gripped him, then quieted. When he breathed deeply, his ribs ached. He pushed past Hackett, looked down the corridor to his left.

Colonel Henry Gibney came weaving down the wide, carpeted hall. He was very drunk. He had a gun in each

111

hand, and his brick-red face was set in an insane expression. There was blood on one cheek. His red, alcoholic eyes focused on Durell and his dirty-white hair was looped thickly over his forehead.

"The Marines have arrived!" he shouted. "How ya, Sam?"

"Hello, Colonel," Durell said.

"You all right, pal?"

"Fine, now."

"Where's m'little Corinne?"

"I don't know," Durell said. "Let's find her. Can you spare a gun for me?"

"Not yet. Gonna shoot me a couple old snakes. Quenton and Hackett. Had enough. Got a gutful. Gonna shoot 'em in the belly and watch the bastards bleed."

"Let's find Corinne first."

"Huh?"

"Corinne," Durell said.

"You seen her?"

"Let's go this way."

Henry Gibney wavered in the hall. Durell walked toward him. His knees felt stiff. He looked back and saw that the door to Quenton's room was closed. Gibney licked his lips and then Durell put a hand on his arm and turned him in the other direction.

"My God," Gibney said. "What happened to you?"

"I've been talking to Hackett all day."

There was no smell of liquor on Gibney's breath.

Durell said, "Where are all the private goons?"

"They won't touch me. They don't dare. Let's find Corinne."

"Right. This way."

Durell went ahead down the hall. A burly, thick-necked man in a gray suit saw them coming and scrambled out of the way, slamming a door. Durell reached the room he had been kept in, opened it, looked inside, closed it again. Someone was shouting out violently angry orders somewhere. From a window, Durell glimpsed the patio and cedar fence that faced the sea. The chairs and tables were empty under the floodlights. No party tonight. No guests.

Corinne was in a room two removed from where he had been kept imprisoned. The entire wing was remote from the main part of the house, connected only by a glassed-in breezeway of abnormal length. He glimpsed another gray-suited guard running across the patio as he opened the door to Corinne's room.

She sat in a wooden chair, facing them. She sat primly, knees together, hands folded in her lap. She wore a shapeless flannel robe.

Gibney's breath hissed. "Good Lord."

"Corinne?" Durell said.

She gave no sign of seeing or hearing.

"Look at her face," Gibney whispered.

He no longer sounded drunk.

They found a side door that led out of the house. Corinne walked between them, moving like an automaton. A chill wind blew from the ocean. Durell tasted salt on his puffed lips. He held Corinne's hand and her fingers were cold and unresponsive. The earth rocked unsteadily under him. He did not try to understand now the riddle of Gibney's appearance. When they reached the sandy dunes that paralleled the beach, he halted.

"Wait. Let Corinne rest," he said.

"I'm all right," Corinne said.

They were the first words she had spoken. He turned to stare sharply at her, and she said dully, "Don't look at me. I don't need a mirror to know how I look. It must be awful. I can see it in your eyes."

"You'll be all right. A good doctor—"

"I don't want a doctor," she said flatly.

Gibney said nervously, "We can't stay here. Let's get on with it, shall we?"

"You came here deliberately, for us?" Durell asked curiously.

"Naturally. Mary insisted."

"Why should you help us?"

"Please," Gibney said. "Mary is waiting."

There was a thickening overcast in the night sky, and the stars were obscured. The cold salt wind made Durell shiver. He looked back at the house. There was no pursuit yet. He wondered what was happening between Quenton and Hackett. Something that held up and confused the chase. The lighted windows made an irregular pattern against the black night. Far up the beach, other windows shone beckoningly.

"They won't let you get away with it," Durell said. "You'll pay for it, Colonel."

"It doesn't matter any more," Gibney said. He breathed, swallowed, breathed again. "They can't hurt me now."

Corinne's head came up. Her face was a grotesque mask in the windy darkness. Her voice was thin. "Henry—have you heard from Roger?"

"Please. Let's start walking. They'll be after us."

They walked on down the beach.

"Have you?" Corinne persisted.

"Yes."

"What is it, Henry? What have you learned?"

Gibney said, "Mary wants to help you, Durell. She says you're not a traitor or a spy at all. God knows how she can guess at these things. I told her she's wrong, that you stole that file to pay me off. She says no. She wants to tell you what you came here to find out. About Quenton and everything else."

Durell felt the slow growth of horror.

"Why are you suddenly willing to do this?"

Corinne said in a high voice, "Is it Roger? Is it?"

"My son is dead," Gibney said. His voice was thick and dull and dusty with despair. "He's been dead for two months."

Corinne stopped walking. She looked at the sea. Durell put a hand on her arm and she pulled away with a quick, savage movement. "Don't touch me!" she whispered.

"Keep going, Corinne. You have to."

"But he's dead!"

"Keep walking, Corinne."

She walked toward the dark line of the surf. Gibney made a strangled sound of dismay. Durell started after her, then halted when the girl paused. He felt helpless. He did not know what he could say to her. He looked back at the house. There was still no pursuit.

"Who told you about your son?" he asked Gibney.

"There was a telephone call. It was from Dickinson Mc-Fee."

"When?"

"Dinnertime. Two hours ago."

"Then it's confirmed?"

"His body was returned to the U.S. military authorities in Berlin last week. It's just been identified by dental records. The date of death was last June—two weeks after he disappeared. The cause was pneumonia. Roger wandered over the line in a delirium of fever and was kept in an East Berlin hospital. So everything that followed afterward was a tissue of lies—the hopes we were given, the betrayal I was forced to make. All lies. And all for nothing. My son is dead."

"I'm sorry," Durell said, knowing his words were inadequate, knowing nothing could compensate this man for the price he had paid and the emptiness lodged in his soul.

"They tricked me. They lied to me," Gibney said.

"Who first approached you?"

"Hackett. And Quenton."

"Hackett *was* your contact?"

"Yes. Please. Let's go. Mary is waiting."

"What does she have to tell me?"

"All about Quenton. She knows where you can get the proof of what he's been doing. Proof enough to destroy him. She says that's what you're really after." Gibney peered up at Durell's face. "That right?"

"Yes," Durell said.

He looked down toward the water for Corinne.

She was gone.

His pulse slowed, then jumped, and he started involuntarily for the darkly ominous surf. Then he saw her running awkwardly toward Quenton's massive house above the beach. He shouted her name at the top of his voice, heedless of danger. She neither slackened her pace nor gave sign that she heard. He took a step or two after her and heard Gibney shout a warning and saw the swift, racing figures of three men who spurted from the house and converged on the running girl. She halted and faced them. There was an odd challenge in the tilt of her head, the stance of her body. Durell checked himself. The three men came together where the girl faced them in the dim light from the house windows. There was a moment of confused motion, soundless under the thunder and crash of the surf. There was another moment of fluidity, then a rapid movement back to the house by one of the men and the girl.

"She's going willingly," Gibney said, wonderingly.

"You know why."

"Should we try to stop her?"

"No," Durell said. "She was in love with your son."

The other two men were coming down the beach toward them, but not too rapidly. He touched Gibney's arm and they moved into the deep shadows of the dunes that barricaded the sea from the marshes inland. He did not think a serious attempt would be made to overtake them.

There are times when you have a choice that is not really a choice at all, he thought, a difference between two paths to follow; but because you are what you are, trained and knowledgeable, you can't even now abandon this cold weighing and balancing of this route or that, of Corinne's life against the information Mary Gibney has for you. It's not a question of doing this first and that afterward. Both are concurrent, and you can accept only one or the other. The pattern is clearer now, and what remains to be done had better be done as fast as you can do it. If Corinne wanted help, she could have asked for it. But is the Corinne who returns placidly to her place of torment and death the same Corinne she was yesterday and the day before? What she was yesterday is forever gone; what she was only a moment ago, before she learned about her Roger, is also gone; and what she is now is the way she chooses to be. And she wants to go back alone. For revenge. For oblivion. Don't follow her. You can't follow her. Your job is in the other direction, and there's no time to waste.

He pushed ahead and did not look back again.

The Gibney house was ordinary compared with the lavish headquarters Quenton had built for himself. It was a ramshackle wooden affair of Victorian vintage, standing alone like something forgotten by time, on a slightly higher dune than those to the south. A veranda encircled the seaward side and there were two turreted wings, and a small beach protected by a sagging palisade. The windows were all dark. Something kept clinking and ringing with a metallic, rhythmic sound, and he saw it was the halyard and metal block on a steel flagpole, swinging back and forth in the chill sea wind, striking the flagpole with quick, impatient tapping sounds.

Gibney paused. He sounded odd. "She was waiting in the library."

"Lights on?"

"Of course."

"Your car still here?"

"Let's look."

It was parked on the sand tracks that led from the island's

main road. The back of the house was dark, too. The wind whipped and crackled in the brush on the dunes. Sand stung Durell's battered face as he turned toward the sea again.

"Let's go in."

"Wait," Gibney said. His voice, normally heavy and booming, recently slurred in deliberate drunken accents, was now pitched high with worry. "Why did she turn off all the lights?"

"Was she alone?"

"Yes. We have no servants here."

"Give me one of your guns," Durell said.

Gibney handed him a Colt .38. The cold metal felt solid and heavy and reassuring. He checked the clip. It was fully loaded.

"Let's find your wife," he said.

The metal pulley clinked loudly on the flagpole as they stepped up on the veranda. The front door stood open. The wind did not seem strong enough to have blown it open. There was nothing but darkness inside. Gibney's face was a pale blob in the gloom. His white hair looked smudged as he stepped over the threshold.

"Mary?" His call was high and thin.

There was no answer.

No one appeared.

There was nothing but the smell of death, strong and ugly in Durell's nostrils.

Gibney made a small keening sound in his throat. He hung back in the open doorway, touched Durell's arm, and Durell felt the shuddering tremors that racked him. "What is it? Where is she, Durell?"

"That room to the left is the library?"

"Yes. She said she'd wait for us there. She told me to get you. She worked it out. She said if I acted drunk enough and wild enough, they wouldn't quite know how to cope with me. And if I found you and dragged you with me, they couldn't actually stop us without violence. She said that Quenton couldn't risk that with me. Quenton wouldn't dare."

His words were a quick, breathless monotone, as if he were trying to dispel and drive away what he knew waited for them in the dark room.

They couldn't wait too long.

"Did you tell anyone else about Roger's death?" Durell asked.

"No. We were alone here when McFee telephoned."

"The call came from Washington?"

"I suppose so."

"Mary took it?"

"Yes."

"When?"

"I'm not sure, really. An hour ago. Maybe longer."

"Weren't you with her when she got the call?"

"I was upstairs. She sat down here alone for perhaps twenty minutes. She was so still, I finally began to wonder about it, and I came down. She looked at me as if she—as if she hated me. I saw at once that she'd been crying. Not making a sound—but crying. She—she had told me how she tried to kill Corinne." Gibney made a plaintive noise. "I know how she hated being so fat. It was a glandular thing with her—it began when Roger was born, when she was pregnant with him. Somehow she never could control it. I guess I—I guess I rather neglected her. I should have tried to understand. . . ."

He was talking as if he already knew she was dead.

Durell went through the doorway, groped on the wall for the light switch, and snapped it on.

chapter SIXTEEN

SHE WAS SEATED ponderously on a wide Victorian settee that faced them, her massive arms resting at her sides, her tiny feet spread the way fat people sit, with knees apart. She wore a voluminous cotton dress that had no shape at all. Durell saw at first no sign of injury except the ugly congestion of her small face. Her eyes were like dark plums protruding from the swollen flesh.

"Mary?" Gibney whispered.

"Don't touch her," Durell said. "You can't help her. Draw the shades."

Gibney was unable to move. There was a decanter on a massive walnut sideboard and Durell found a glass and poured bourbon into it and handed it to Gibney. The man downed it as if it were water. He stared without comprehension at his dead wife, while Durell examined the woman more closely. He still could not determine the cause of death. Then his attention was caught by a small loop of wire that dangled from under her long pale hair at the nape of her neck. Very gingerly he lifted the heavy mass of hair and saw how the wire had been looped around the woman's throat and drawn so tightly that it was buried in the double and triple layers of fat on Mary Gibney's neck. She had been strangled with efficiency. It had happened to her without warning. There had been no time for any sort of struggle.

He looked gravely at Gibney. "Who knew that you were going to try to get me out of Quenton's place?"

"Nobody. Nobody *could* have known!"

"Could anyone have listened to McFee's call, here on the island?"

"I don't know. I don't think so. It's a private line."

"Quenton doesn't have it tapped?"

"I doubt it. I checked."

"Nobody else was in the house when Mary said she wanted to give me the dope on Quenton?"

"We were alone. Mary and I—we were alone." Gibney's voice was a hoarse whisper. His florid face was now yellow and waxen. "And now she's truly alone. Out there, somewhere. I wasn't very good to her. I—I thought I hated her. But we—long ago, before Roger was born—she was beautiful. She was wonderful. We shared so many things. . . ."

"Stop it," Durell said harshly. "We have to think of now, this moment."

Gibney stared without understanding. Durell listened. The wind shook the old house, made wood creak, thumped a shutter lightly. No other sounds. But he had the feeling they were not alone. His eyes ranged the Victorian room: he sensed the mildew caused by the salt air, the pungency of bourbon in Gibney's glass. Nothing. Then where was the danger? It was here, somewhere. He thought of the two guards who had plunged after them when Corinne turned back to Quenton's. They should have arrived by now. But they were not here. His nerves quivered.

"Do you have a car, Henry? Can we get off the island?"

Gibney looked into his glass, put it down, and took his gun from his pocket. His voice was flat. "We couldn't possibly make it. There's only the one road. Quenton's phony cops would stop us."

"A boat, then?"

Gibney shook his head. "I don't own a boat."

"But there should be at least one, somewhere on the island!" Durell said savagely. "Think, man!"

"There's an auxiliary ketch. I think it belongs to one of Hackett's men—fellow named Killian. No better than the rest of them."

"Where is it? Damn it, help me!"

"At the inlet, other side of the island. Maybe a quarter of a mile." Gibney seemed uninterested. He sank to his knees before his dead wife and took one of the fat, dimpled hands and kissed it. "Mary," he whispered. "Mary, I'm so sorry!"

Durell moved to the door, snapped off the light, plunged the room into darkness. Gibney struggled to his feet in surprise.

"What are you doing?"

"How do I get to that boat?"

"I told you. Straight across the island. But we can't leave Mary alone like this, in the dark!"

There came a stumbling, crashing sound as Gibney got up and then fell over some article of furniture.

At the same time, from down the beach, came the sound of two shots, spaced briefly, distinct and deliberate.

Corinne, Durell thought.

The sea wind blew cold from the east. He stepped out on the veranda, looked to the right at the dim aureole of light from Quenton's house. The tall dune grass rattled and clicked and cast dim shadows amid the deeper darkness. Here and there a star gleamed through the overcast. His mind jumped ahead, across the island, to the boat Gibney had described. They would be busy at Quenton's place, with Corinne. The causeway to the island would be effectively sealed off, and they wouldn't be worried about his escape in that direction. Would they think of the boat, too? Maybe. It was a chance, a calculated risk. He could not afford capture again. He had to get off the island at once. Gibney and Corinne were no longer important. He was through weighing one against the other, this life against that. Not when a tiny flame thousands of miles from here could suddenly flare into a holocaust that might consume the world.

He stepped down the path toward the road. Gibney was still in the house, weeping over his dead wife. He had good cause to weep. There was no road back from the place where he had gone.

Shadows moved in the brush beside the driveway. Gibney's car was parked here. He ignored it and watched the shadows. Only the wind. Or was it? He walked with a long stride, sensing weakness in him from his long hours with Hackett. His strength was limited. There was danger around him. When he reached the main road he stopped abruptly and spun around, looking backward. The dark waves of the dunes seemed to be moving after him. The house was cloaked in blackness.

When he turned back to the road, he saw the car directly ahead of him, silent, waiting, without lights. He took two steps and halted again. The moon shone briefly through the shredding overcast. There was an official government license on the sedan. Beyond the road, he saw a dim path that twisted across the dunes on the landward side of the island, and beyond that was a small shed, about four hundred feet away, and the masts of a boat tied to a dock out in the salt-water inlet. Much farther away, all but lost in the haze of night, was a scatter of dim house lights like a handful of scattered jewels.

He walked toward the car ahead, gripped by a sudden fatalism, and when he was perhaps fifteen feet from it, the door opened and a man stepped out holding a gun and said, "That will be all, Sam."

It was Burritt Swayney.

There was no surprise left in Durell. Swayney's voice was thick and satisfied, silky smooth, like the glisten of oil on the gun he carried. Durell halted. He kept his own gun lowered.

"How did you get here, Burritt?"

"There seems to be some confusion on the island. Throw your gun into the brush."

Durell threw his gun away. He saw where it landed and looked at Swayney. The chief of K Section, small and fat, seemed no different than he had looked yesterday morning in his office at Number 20 Annapolis Street—trim, tidy, priggish, swollen with triumph.

"Come over here now. Got any other weapons, Sam?"

"No."

"You've kicked up a lot of dust."

"I'm not through yet," Durell said.

"Oh, yes, you are. Quite through. I'm taking you back with me. On the other hand, if you bat an eyelash, I'll shoot to kill. Believe that, Sam."

"I believe it."

"Where is the girl?"

"Corinne? With Quenton, I think."

"And Gibney?"

"In his house."

"Who killed his wife, Sam?"

Durell grinned tightly. "Maybe you can tell me, Burritt."

Swayney smiled without meaning. His round face glistened with sweat, although the sea wind was cool. He wore his gray suit and prissy little bow tie and his small mouth pursed and stretched and pursed again. His head jerked briefly from right to left. The road was empty.

"You've led our security people a merry chase, Sam. All hell broke loose when you flipped the loyalty board. Everybody breathing down my neck over you, you bastard. I swore I'd get you personally. What were you doing here? Tell me, Sam."

"I'll tell Dickinson McFee."

"Nest of spies, hey? Pals of yours?"

"You can make what you want out of it."

"I'll make plenty, don't you worry, you Cajun bastard. How come you're running around loose?"

"You said it yourself, Burritt," Durell told him quietly. "There's been some trouble here. Murder and mayhem. How did you get aboard?"

"No guards. I took the chance. Turned out good, hey?"

"You've been here before, Burritt?"

"Once or twice."

"As a pal of Senator Quenton?"

"Get in the car, Sam. I'm taking you into custody."

"All right," Durell said. "Just answer one thing. What made you come here alone? And how did you know about Mary Gibney?"

"I was just in the house. And I don't need any help to handle you, Sam."

"Why were you so sure I was here?"

Swayney smirked. He gestured with the gun. His pudgy figure looked tense. "You forget what makes me good at my job. I don't need any calculators or dossiers to know about the people in K Section. I can quote chapter and verse on the histories of more folks than you ever knew. I knew Corinne worked for Q in our section, but as long as her activities were relatively harmless, I didn't interfere. Better a known danger than an unknown. I knew about Gibney's connections with Quenton and Hackett, too. All about it. Chapter and verse. I finally put two and two together and came here to pick you up. Feather in my cap. Might take over McFee's job."

"Just like that?"

"Get in the car, Sam. Last time I ask you."

"All right," Durell said. "You and I can do business."

"No. I don't do business with traitors like you."

"Then let's go back to Washington. We'll talk about it."

Something glistened in Swayney's pale eyes. Durell read temptation, and a moment's indecision. It was enough. Swayney glanced beyond him at the house on the beach, and then Durell moved, without mercy. He hit Swayney hard. Swayney screamed like a woman and the gun went off, smashing a bullet into the sandy road. Durell hit him again, closed a hand around Swayney's smooth wrist, and flung the stout man against the car. Swayney screamed again. His eyes reflected fear of immediate death.

"Sam, don't!"

Durell hit him a third time, saw the gun spin to the road, and kicked it aside. Swayney sprawled on the sand, arms and legs kicking in a feeble swimming gesture. Durell reached into the car, plucked the ignition key from the lock, and hurled it into the brush. His stomach churned. He drew a deep, steadying breath and looked down the road toward Quenton's house and saw someone running toward him.

It was Corinne.

He did not question her appearance. He moved to meet her, seeing her bruised and battered face in a shred of moon-light that prodded down through the wind-torn clouds.

"Sam . . . help me. They're coming."

"What did you do?"

She gasped in great, shuddering breaths, her mouth opening darkly. "Tried to kill . . . Quenton . . . for Roger."

"Did you?"

"No. I couldn't. Oh, please, they're coming now!"

He looked at Swayney, crawling away on the ground, and he looked toward the sea and the Victorian house where Henry Gibney knelt beside the massive bulk of his dead wife. He took Corinne's hand and together they ran across the dunes toward the boat shed and the yawl that waited for them.

chapter SEVENTEEN

DAWN HAD COME. Durell had slept for two hours, but the first brightening of the sky touched him and woke him all at once. Sea gulls cried plaintively in the marshes, and the surface of the Chesapeake was a vast mirror touched with all the pinks and golds and blues of the new day. The ketch was hidden in a salt-water creek miles behind them. Somebody would find it soon, he thought slowly, and then the chase would be on again.

Corinne was still asleep in the haystack beside him, and he winced when he looked at the dark wreckage of her face. She would never be beautiful again. She had found slacks and a sweater on the ketch, and her proud body looked oddly crumpled in the misfitting garments. She had no shoes. Yet she had not whimpered or complained through the long hours after he had run the ketch into its hiding place. She had walked beside him in numb silence, hiding her face, saying little. He wondered what had given her this new impetus to escape and live. There was a hard bravery in her, a refusal to surrender, that could be her salvation in this most bitter hour she had ever known. He felt shaken by a deep pity for her.

"Corinne," he said gently.

She opened her eyes, discolored and bruised, and made

a moaning sound. He saw that she did not comprehend where they were or how they had reached this sloping field by the edge of the bay. Then all at once the recall came and her hands flew to cover her features.

"Don't—don't look at me," she whispered.

"You'll be all right. We'll get you to a doctor today."

"No, no, he couldn't help. But you need a doctor yourself." She sat up, her head turned away from him. "Where are we?"

"Upriver from the boat. There's a highway just past this farm. I've heard cars on it."

"It's going to be a hot day," she said. But she shivered. "What will we do? I think, whatever you plan for yourself, you will be better off without me."

"Nonsense." He helped her to her feet. Her mouth went white as she attempted a few steps and fell to her knees. He caught her and held her erect against him. Her breath hissed. "I'm sorry."

"We'll find a car, or a truck."

"It's no use. They won't let us get far."

"Start walking."

"Sam, I can't!"

He slapped her. The sting of his open palm against her battered face shocked great tears in her puffed and discolored eyes. A little cry of animal anguish crept from her throat.

"Come on," he said. "Don't quit now, Corinne."

"How can you be so cruel?"

"I have to be. Let's go."

They moved slowly, walking in silent pain across the newly mown hayfield. The light brightened in the east. The bay turned into molten gold for a brief moment, and over a rise Durell saw the reflected light from an aluminum barn roof. He headed that way as a cock began to crow, and from far off up the shore came the sound of a motorboat.

A small pickup truck was parked beside the barn. The house itself was across the road beyond a row of tall oaks that hid them from its view. Durell leaned the girl against the tail gate of the truck and looked for the keys. They were lying on the worn leather seat, and he cursed the darkness of last night that had made him halt so near to this means of escape.

"In you go," he told Corinne.

She looked at him with helpless eyes. "I want to die."

"Not yet," he said harshly. "There are some things we want to do first, you and I. Remember Roger?"

"I want to forget. I want to sleep. I want to die."

"Are you hungry?"

"No. Yes."

"Thirsty?"

"Yes."

He grinned. "There you are, then. Come on."

She saw the grin and tried to smile back and her shoulders straightened slightly. "You are too good to me."

"And we're wasting precious time."

Five minutes later they were on the Washington road, rolling at forty miles an hour across the dawning Virginia countryside.

At six o'clock he found an open service station at a crossroad, flanked by a diner and a bus stop. He pulled into the back lot behind the grease racks and told Corinne to go into the ladies' room and clean up. He doused water on his bearded face in the rest room, wincing at the mirror. Searching his pockets, he found some crumpled, water-soaked bills and a few coins. He bought a pocket comb and a handkerchief, soaked his head under the tap, and held the handkerchief to his face when another patron came in. Outside, he waited at the truck until Corinne reappeared and gave her the handkerchief and comb.

"It's hopeless, isn't it?" she murmured. "How far can we get? And where are we *going?*"

"We're getting a doctor for you."

"And if the police take us?"

"They won't," he said, with a confidence he did not feel. "Now clean yourself up."

"My nose is broken," she said dully. "And two teeth. I am ugly."

"Anything else?"

"Inside. I don't know. Hackett did it."

He had no answer. A bus hissed to a stop at the diner up the road. He looked at it thoughtfully, and at the truck. A state police car slammed by, moving at high speed, heading back toward the shore. At the same moment the gas-station attendant came walking toward them.

Durell took Corinne's arm. "Walk naturally."

"Hey, you!"

Durell looked over his shoulder. "Yeah?"

"That your truck?"

"No," Durell said.

"Where's the guy drove it in here?"

"How would I know?"

He turned and walked toward the diner with Corinne before the attendant got a good look at their faces. The bus was almost loaded, but there were two empty seats available. Corinne kept her face averted while Durell bought tickets from the driver.

"What in hell happened to you?" the driver asked.

"Accident."

"You and the lady look in pretty rough shape, mister."

"Are you going to Alexandria?"

"Sure. But you oughta go to a hospital."

They took a seat directly behind the driver, rather than face the curious stares of the other passengers. Now and then Durell looked up to meet the driver's puzzled eyes in the mirror. Corinne found a newspaper on the seat and held it up before her face.

No good, Durell thought. You should have stayed with the truck. But the truck was hot by now, reported stolen, and both Quenton and Swayney would be alert for any report that might indicate where they could be found. The area of search would necessarily be small, once they found the ketch. The certainty that there would be road-blocks up ahead grew stronger, and with that certainty came a heavy weight of despair.

He moved ahead through instinct, impelled by the pressure of increasing danger. Corinne was a burden, sapping his depleted strength, a dead weight that he did not once consider abandoning. The way ahead was like an interminable desert; his goal of vindication for himself and the exposure of a wide looming menace that threatened all he loved and held dear seemed like a chimera seen vaguely through a glaze of heat. His training dictated the moves he made: debarking from the bus at a small town below Alexandria; a visit to the drugstore for bandages and heavy make-up for Corinne's face; the ride on a local train, filled with commuters buried in their morning papers; the interminable starts and stops; the glimpse of the Potomac, the glimmer of Washington in the distance. Corinne was in a stupor of exhaustion and pain. It was like a trip through hell, carried out on the dragging feet of the damned.

A taxi took them to the address he gave, far out in the sprawling Maryland suburbs of the capital, and it was after ten o'clock when they halted a block from Art Greenwald's apartment.

Calculated risk, he thought.

There was a time to stand alone, and a time to call for help. He did not know if his appeal would be answered. He paid off the cab with the last of his currency and helped Corinne to the sidewalk. The girl leaned heavily against him. If the cabby was curious, he contained himself, accepted his tip, and drove off, not too fast, not too slow. The street was quiet, sunny, deserted.

"Can you walk to the corner?" he asked Corinne.

Her face was like a grotesque mask under the bandages and the make-up. Her breathing was quick and shallow, and her hand on his arm felt cool and wet.

"Corinne?"

"Yes, Roger," she mumbled. "I'm coming, darling."

He checked a reply and began walking toward the red-brick colonial apartment house where Art Greenwald lived. A milk truck went by on silent tires. A baby wailed. He knew he should be on the lookout for an official visitor at Art's, but it was too late for caution now.

The lobby felt cool, and when he rang the bell he leaned against the stone wall, supporting Corinne, and he did not hear the answering buzz until it was twice repeated. The Greenwald apartment was on the third floor, reached by a self-service elevator. When he helped Corinne into the upper hallway, he saw Rosalie Greenwald in the open doorway of her flat.

As the slight, dark-haired woman recognized him, surprise gave way to bright hatred in her wide brown eyes.

chapter EIGHTEEN

DURELL SUPPORTED Corinne with the last of his strength. A wave of darkness washed over him. "Help her," he told Rosalie.

The small, dark-haired woman looked incredulous. "What are you doing here?"

"I've got to see Art."

"There's nothing here for you. Nothing you can say to Art. You tried to kill him, and he thought you were his best friend."

"Is that what Art says?"

"No, but—"

"For God's sake, let us in!".

Art Greenwald's deep voice came querulously from an inner room. Rosalie bit her lip. She looked at Corinne with dawning astonishment, shock, pity. "My dear . . ."

She helped Durell carry her inside. The apartment was small, comfortably furnished, chintzy. The shades were drawn against the mounting morning heat. There was the smell of fresh coffee, of bacon and eggs; and he saw that Rosalie wore a kitchen apron on which she nervously dried her hands.

"Put her in Mother's room. It's all right—she's gone to Philadelphia. I'll call a doctor."

"Wait until I see Art. We need one we can trust."

"Do the police still want you?"

Durell nodded. "Corinne, too."

"What—what happened to her?"

"Some people asked her a few questions—with gestures."

Rosalie licked her full lips. "And you?"

"Same thing. Not so bad."

They were interrupted as Durell helped Corinne into bed. Art Greenwald stood in pajamas, his arm and shoulder in crisp white bandages. "Sam! For God's sake, Sam!"

Durell gave him a level stare. "I had no other place to go, Art. I need help. The girl needs care."

"It's all right, Sam."

"You have a choice," Durell said. "You can call the cops or McFee, if you feel you should. I won't stop you now."

"Ah, shut up!"

"I hate to bring the risk of trouble to you this way."

"You crazy Cajun, I don't know what you're doing or why, but it's all right with me. Rosalie?"

Art's wife looked up sharply from Corinne's limp figure on the bed. Her face was ashen, and horror crawled in her normally gentle eyes. "What kind of people did this to that poor girl?"

"People I'm after," Durell said. "I'm going to get them. I know how to do it now. But I need help. You can help me, Art. It's important. We can—"

"Right now you need to hit the sack."

"I don't think there's time."

"You're dead beat," Art said grimly. "You can use my bed. I'll get Doc Frye to look at both of you. I'll tell him it's departmental and confidential business. He'll keep quiet about it."

Durell felt the room slowly turning underfoot. There was no further resistance in him. He heard Rosalie's sudden cry of alarm as he slid down into a cool place of darkness that had been waiting for him. . . .

He awoke to see a stranger wearing glasses standing over him, and he felt the prick of a needle in his arm.

"How is the girl, Doctor?"

"How do you feel?"

"I want to get up."

"The girl may be all right. Art tells me not to ask questions. But it seems to me you've been dealing with savages."

"Yes," Durell said.

"Get some sleep. You're exhausted. Nothing else serious."

"Is Art around? I've got to—"

The face withdrew, the room darkened, and he slept. He heard voices now and then, and gradually he dreamed, and he was with Deirdre in a strange place, a plain that stretched from horizon to horizon, arid and endless as far as the eye could see. At least, he thought it was Deirdre, until she turned to face him with the slow pirouette of a ballet dancer, and he saw the bloody, evil mask she wore over her face. He cried out and struck at the loathsome mask, and she laughed and ran away from him. Her laughter was the tinkling of silver bells that echoed to the wide, naked horizon. He chased her. From out of the dry, dusty earth sprang a chain of naked men and women, all masked, holding hands and barring his way as he tried to follow Deirdre. Their laughter built a wall of battering waves against him. He looked from a silver mask to a gold mask to one that dripped great gouts of blood. Deirdre was lost among all these masked, nude people. Overhead, the sun turned blue and then red and burned down upon his head with an intolerable weight. The chattering clamor from the masked people had the unreal, parrotty quality of a flight of birds. He could not see Deirdre's mask among them. He shouted at the grotesque horrors that leered and jeered at him. Something struck him lightly across the chest. It was a whip. The lashing sting came again, and then something exploded in his eyes and his hands came up instinctively, clawing at his face, and he felt the unreality of the mask that covered his face, too. . . .

He awoke, sweating, trembling, a scream dying in his throat.

Deirdre sat beside the bed, and for a moment he was confused between the dream and reality. The room was dimly lighted. It was hot. Deirdre was not aware of his wakening, and he did not move, watching her as his mind cleared and the nightmare faded. She sat quietly in a slipper chair, hands in repose on her lap, her dark-red hair gleaming in the subdued light of the bedside lamp. She wore a print cotton suit of lime-colored twill, and a dark-green pin glinted on her lapel. She looked cool and composed, except for the small frown incised between the delicate wings of her brows. She was listening to Rosalie's voice in muted argument coming from another room in the apartment.

Durell stirred and she looked quickly at him, anxiety at once evident in her wide eyes, in the touch of her hand on his stubbled cheek.

"Sam? You were dreaming. . . ."

"How did you get here?"

"Art called me, through Sidonie. He told me how you showed up here with Corinne this morning. How do you feel?"

"Not too bad. And Corinne?"

"Under a sedative. How did that happen to her, Sam?"

He had no wish to tell her. "What time is it?"

She looked at the small gold watch he had given her for her birthday, a month ago; it seemed as if that day and time belonged to another century on another planet. "It's nine-thirty."

"Nobody followed you here?"

"I was very careful. I've been here for hours."

"I'm grateful."

She smiled. "You're going to make it all right, aren't you?"

"As soon as I've showered and shaved and eaten."

"The doctor says you're to stay in bed until tomorrow."

"Tomorrow may be too late." He swung his legs over the edge of the bed, winced as numerous bruises made their presence known, and felt the pull and strain of stiffened muscles all through his body. Rosalie's voice ended abruptly, as if she had heard the bed creak. Durell saw that fresh clothing for him had been folded over a nearby chair. "Ask Rosalie to make some coffee," he suggested. "I'll only be ten minutes."

Deirdre was concerned. "Are you sure you're all right?"

He kissed her, meaning to be brief, but her lips clung to his and her arms held him tight with a desperate embrace and he felt a trembling go through her. "I was so afraid for you," she whispered. "Sam, darling—you drove me away deliberately, didn't you?"

"I had to," he said. A weight lifted from him. "It was best."

Her eyes were shining. "And it's all right now?"

"We'll make it all right."

"I want to help," she said.

"And I need your help. Get the coffee going."

Ten minutes later he sat in the kitchen with the shades drawn, freshly shaved, showered, dressed in the clothing Deirdre had brought for him. The sleep induced by the doctor's sedative had helped him. He knew that the stiffness and aches in him would work out shortly. Rosalie, at the window, watched him with a measure of reservation in her dark eyes. Now and then she looked quickly at Art, as if unable to understand Art's unhesitating acceptance of what Durell was saying. Durell, as he told them what he wanted to do and what help he would need, felt a lift of gladness that the nightmare of outcast loneliness was almost over. He was not alone.

These were his friends, who believed in what he was and had been. In Art there was loyalty; in Deirdre there was love. Not alone, he told himself. Not ever. You can put on all sorts of masks, but those who truly know you will always recognize you and speak your name to you in tones of friendship.

Art was frowning. "Sam, I don't know how we can swing it. You know what security is like at Number Twenty."

"I've got to get in there," Durell said.

"And the missing file?"

"We get that first."

"Suppose it isn't where you think it is?"

"It can't be anywhere else. I'll need your car, Art."

"Sure."

"When does the night guard on the roof come on? At twelve?"

"This week, yes." Art nodded.

"Then we have two hours. Give me the car keys."

"Uh-uh. I'll drive."

Durell nodded. "Deirdre?"

"I'm coming, too."

He looked up at Rosalie and wondered why Art's wife said nothing. "Rosalie, will you call McFee at exactly twelve-fifteen? No sooner, no later."

"Yes," she said.

chapter NINETEEN

ART'S CAR was a three-year-old Chevrolet sedan, dusty and worn by shopping trips and children's restless feet. Durell sat beside Deirdre as Art drove. The road was familiar. Here was where it had started, forty-eight hours ago, on this winding Virginia country lane. Here was where he had first spotted the following car, and up there was the white barricade where the bridge was washed out. And there was the ravine, just beyond. Memory flooded back and he saw again the terror in Corinne's eyes as they fled into the brush before their silent pursuers. Here was where it started to go wrong. Here he could begin to set it right.

The lane was deserted. Katydids sang and crickets shrilled in the treetops. Moonlight made a quicksilver pattern on the tiny stream far below. Durell got out of the car, followed by Deirdre and Art.

"This where you were slugged?" Art asked.

"A little farther down the slope. The envelope should be in the brush down there, between that clump of bushes and the bottom of the ravine. It hasn't rained since, so it ought to be all right."

"Jesus, I hope so," Art said. "But we could use a dozen men to search this place and do it right."

Each of them had a flashlight. Durell went sliding down to the clump of birches where he had been trapped. There were still traces of trampled brush and flattened grass where they had struggled. He flicked the flashlight here and there. Nothing. A white stone gleamed and his pulse jumped until he discovered it was just a stone. No envelope. He circled wider, using a pattern with Art and Deirdre. Their lights poked and prodded and swept in tight, jabbing circles. The brush was dark and forbidding. The katydids sang. Below, the creek chuckled over smooth rocks.

Nothing.

For twenty minutes he worked his way back and forth across the steep slope, moving downward reluctantly, tracing the path he had made when he slipped and rolled down to the edge of the creek two nights ago. Here and there a broken branch, a trampled shrub showed him the path he had followed. He listened to the swift run of the creek. White water frothed at his feet. This was where he had come to and found Jones, the M.I. man, and Amos Hackett standing over him. He was sure this was the spot. And he had found nothing.

Corinne didn't have it, Gibney didn't have it, Hackett didn't have it. It had to be here. But it wasn't here.

Art came up to him, lowering his light. "Sam?"

"This is the place," Durell said.

"Your pocket was ripped? The one you put the file in?"

"It fell out when I fell downhill."

"How long were you out?"

"Half an hour. Maybe more."

"Could they have moved you, carried you somewhere else?"

"I don't know," Durell said. He pulled himself together. "We'll keep looking. Deirdre, you and Art go downstream. I'll see what's up above. We'll take another half hour."

He knew he was groping in the dark; and he saw no light ahead.

The sound of a gushing waterfall touched him a few moments later. The steep banks of the ravine fell away and the brush thinned, revealing the gentle roll of a wide field, placid under the moonlight. The waterfall was only ten feet high, and a narrow wooden footbridge spanned the creek above. Durell looked back. The probing gleam of Deirdre's light was lost to sight. He climbed the bank, feeling the cold spray against his face, and crossed the footbridge.

The figure of a man or a boy stood on the opposite bank, waiting for him.

"All right, mister. Stand where you are!"

Durell halted. Moonlight traced a liquid finger on the barrel of a shotgun pointed at him.

"Where are your friends?" he was asked.

"Downstream."

"Find what you're looking for?"

Durell drew a deep breath. "Not yet."

"Come over here. Slow and easy. You got a gun, you better not go for it. I can pick off a crow at a hundred feet. I ain't braggin', because my dad tells me never to brag. It's just a fact, mister. Be careful."

"All right," Durell said.

Moonlight touched the other's face. A boy, about seventeen, in blue denims and checked shirt, a long-billed blue naval cap pushed back over dark hair. A grim, youthful face. He stood with his feet apart, balanced on a shelf of rock above the footpath. Beyond him, the lights of a farmhouse gleamed on the other side of the field.

"I been watching for you since last night, mister."

"You found my envelope?"

"It ain't yours," said the boy. "It's the government's. A rat like you, I ought to fill your belly with shot. I seen your picture in the papers. Dad saw it, too. Lucky I was down here huntin' for crows. I hunt a lot. I'm a good shot. I found what you're lookin' for, mister."

"Good," Durell said.

"You might change your mind. Put your hands behind your neck and march, mister."

"Don't get excited," Durell said evenly.

The boy said resentfully, "I told Dad you'd show up. I told him I was bound to be right about you. And here you are."

"Have you turned the envelope over to the police yet?"

"Shut up. Walk ahead of me."

"Gladly," Durell said.

The path followed a clump of oaks beside the creek, then skirted the field toward the farm that lay peacefully under the August moon. The boy trudged doggedly at his heels, and Durell did not need to turn around to know that the shotgun was aimed at the small of his back. He felt elation, suppressed it; he had been right, but he didn't have the file yet.

The farmhouse was sprawling, with freshly painted barns and sheds across the dooryard, well-kept fences, and the smell of hay and silage in the hot night air. Lights glowed in the windows. A horse nickered in the nearby pasture. Durell paused. "Where now?"

"Inside. They're waiting for you."

His elation faded. "Who is waiting?"

"The government people. They came at suppertime." The youngster grinned tightly. "What's the matter, mister? Scared of what Uncle Sam is gonna do to you for being a lousy spy?"

"What's your name?" Durell asked suddenly.

"Tommy. Tom Henderson."

"Your father runs this farm?"

"Sure. I told you—"

"Anybody else in the family?"

"Mom. My kid brother. I found the envelope yesterday, like I said. Dad kept it and finally called the people you used to work for."

Durell turned in the face of the shotgun. His intense manner threw the boy off guard. "Who, exactly, did he call?"

"I dunno," the boy muttered. "Your boss, I think."

"General McFee?"

"I dunno, I tell you. Now get—"

Durell jumped. The boy wasn't quite ready for it. He knocked the shotgun aside and slammed a forearm across the boy's white face. Tommy went bowling over into the dust. The shotgun did not go off. The boy started to yell and Durell applied the pressure of a thumb against the boy's throat and Tommy's eyes bugged and the sound died strangling in his larynx.

"Listen to me," Durell gasped. "Are you listening?"

A frantic nod.

"I'm not going to hurt you. I don't want to hurt you or your family, understand? I'm not a spy. Not a traitor. If there are people waiting in your house for me, it's they that betrayed our country. Do you believe that?"

The boy's eyes glittered. He did not believe it. Without releasing his grip, Durell found the shotgun with his free hand and dragged it to his side. "When I let go, don't yell. I'm desperate. I'll kill you if you make a sound."

The boy made a spitting, choking noise.

Durell eased his grip. Tommy drew a great shuddering breath. His eyes hated Durell. Durell leveled the shotgun at Tommy Henderson.

"Believe me," he said quietly.

"Lousy traitor," Tommy whispered.

A screen door whined and slammed. A man stood in the fan of light spraying the front porch; his head was thrust forward in an attitude of listening and searching. One of Quenton's guards. Durell raked the boy's ribs lightly with the shotgun in warning. The guard looked this way and that and then went inside, letting the door slam again.

"Who was that?" Durell whispered.

"One of the FBI guys."

"He's not. He's one of the thugs we've been fighting. Did your dad give them the envelope?"

"I don't know."

"If he did, why are they still here?"

"I wouldn't know."

"How long have you been out of the house?"

"I told you. Since after supper."

"Did you tell them why you went to the creek?"

Tommy looked sullen and sheepish. "Nope. I wanted to do this myself." His eyes glittered with tears of frustration. "You spoiled it."

Durell studied the house. At that moment a high, thin scream of anguish came from a lower window at the rear. It was instantly cut off, but the boy heard it, too. He made a noise in his throat.

"What was that?"

"I hope I'm wrong, but I don't think so," Durell whispered. "That was your father."

"But—"

"They're questioning him about the envelope."

"Listen, they can't—"

Durell slapped the boy lightly. He stood shaking, teeth clenched. Big freckles stood out against his young face. Sweat shone on his cheeks. The scream was not repeated. A shadow moved quickly across a window and was gone. Durell drew a deep breath. The shotgun was smooth and solid and comfortable in his grip.

"I'm going to see," the boy said suddenly.

"Wait!"

Durell's words checked him before he quit the shadow of the barn. He stood shaking. "If they've hurt Dad or Mom—"

"Make up your mind to it. They've been hurt. But it won't help if you barge in now. I'll go in. But you wait for my friends."

"Friends?"

"They're downstream. They'll be following me up here soon. Go back to the bridge and meet them. Tell them I'm in the house with the Q men."

"Q?"

"They'll understand. *Go on!*"

Durell shoved him toward the field. The boy ran stumbling, paused, looked back, licked his lips. Then suddenly he began to sprint as hard as he could toward the distant line of trees that marked the creek and the ravine they had come from.

Durell turned to the house.

chapter TWENTY

A whimpering came from the dark.

It was the sound a strong man makes when he balances at the uttermost limit of his endurance—a sound midway between a choked scream and a final, despairing yell of defiance.

Durell listened for it again, but there were only murmurous voices from the other side of the farmhouse. He stood in blackness on the back porch, flat against the wall. He heard a woman speak, pleading. Her words were followed by a sharp slap, a mutter of rage. She pleaded again. She offered anything, anything. She spoke to someone named John, begging him to tell them.

The whimpering broke through again, ceased, came again.

"Soon," someone said. "But where is that damned brat?"

"Out joy-riding, I guess."

"I'd rather have him here."

"Don't worry about it."

"I can't waste more time at this!"

"What you want is somewhere in the house. He'll tell us."

"He's dying. Where is the boy?"

Then, coaxingly: "Tell us, John. Tell us. You'll die. He'll die. Your wife will die. Tell us, man. Speak up."

Whimpering came through the darkness.

Someone stood on guard just inside the screened door from the back porch. Durell felt his presence there was a tangible block to his entry. He felt time running away through his fingers. The shotgun felt hot and slippery in his hand.

He scratched lightly at the door.

Someone said, "That you, Amos?"

"Come on out," Durell said softly.

"What in hell?"

The shadow stepped out, the door whined, slammed. Durell struck. The man slumped, folded over the porch rail. Durell did not look at him. He stepped inside.

He was in the kitchen. Light shone in a hallway ahead, where the sounds of torment crawled in the air. Durell moved silently in that direction. The woman's voice lifted again, murmuring, pleading. He smelled cigar smoke, heavy and fragrant in the dead air. His stomach crawled. He sweated. He lifted the shotgun to his hip and walked into the room ahead just as the man in there screamed his way onto a high plane of anguish and fell away.

"Drop it," Durell said from the doorway.

A white-haired man in blue denim overalls stared up from a wooden chair. His eyes looked blind in his weathered face. There were two other men in the room. One was Hereward Quenton. The other was Hackett. In a corner, huddled in a rocker with her knuckles in her mouth, biting on them until blood ran down her hand, was a middle-aged woman wearing a plain cotton house dress.

Quenton made a strangling sound.

"Get your gun, Amos," Durell said. He did not recognize his own voice. He was shaking. "Go ahead, reach for it."

"You'd kill me," Hackett said in a kind of wonderment.

"That's right."

"Mister?" the woman asked feebly. "Mister, that's my boy's gun."

"Tommy is all right," Durell said, not looking at her.

Hackett's mouth crawled and twitched in his saturnine face. He stared in fascination at the shotgun. He stared at Durell. He shuddered.

Durell said to the woman, "Get your husband some water."

"But they'll—"

"Go ahead. No, wait. Are there any other men here?"

"One. One in the kitchen."

"No others?"

"I don't think so."

"Go ahead, then."

She got up, still biting her knuckles, and hurried out. Quenton sank down into the rocking chair. He looked like a shriveled mummy. His flaccid cheeks were gray and pinched. His eyes were like dead glass beads in his face. His mouth was a dark hole in which his tongue flicked from one corner to the other. He looked obscene.

"You made a mistake," Durell told him, "in coming here with Hackett. I imagine you usually give a wide berth to the jobs Hackett does for you. But you had to be in on this one, didn't you?"

Quenton made unintelligible sounds. His tongue flicked back and forth on rubbery lips.

"Did Henderson tell you where to find the file?" Durell asked.

"No. No."

"But he has it, right?"

"Yes. Right. Yes, he has it."

"You want it badly, eh?"

Something flickered to life in the glass-bead eyes. The twangy drawl quickened. "Real bad, son. Real bad. I could use it. I need it. I'll pay plenty for it. Look here, son, I don't know how you got here, but—"

"Don't call me son," Durell said.

"I mean—I'll pay you good. I'm rich. You don't know how rich. Hackett made a mistake. I should've hired you. I could've bought you into my side, couldn't I? Sure I could. You told me you're for sale. That's right, isn't it?"

"No," Durell said.

"No?" Blank eyes stared at him.

"Is that so hard to believe?"

The woman came back, carrying a tray of medicines, bandages, water, and some washcloths. She hesitated, looked at Durell. "I'm frightened for my husband. He needs a doctor. The things that man did—"

"Which man?"

She pointed at Hackett. "Him," she whispered.

Hackett looked satanic, his dark curly hair in ringlets over his flat forehead. His eyes flickered, flashed, grew opaque like the eyes of a reptile, filmed over by retreating thought.

"Fix him up, Amos," Durell ordered. "Give him those things, ma'am."

"I don't want him to touch John."

"It will be all right. There's a man on the back porch. Can you get some clothesline and tie him up so he won't get free again?"

She nodded mutely. Then her face crumpled.

"What is it?" he asked. "Is there anything more?"

"Just—thank you. Thank you for coming here."

"You can help me, Mrs. Henderson," Durell said. "Do you know where my envelope is?"

"No. John called somebody in Washington when Tommy found those papers, and then he put them somewhere until these men came."

"Whom did he call? Was it General McFee?"

She nodded anxiously. "Yes, that was the name."

"And then these men arrived?"

She nodded again, quickly, her eyes darting from Quenton to Hackett and then to her dazed, bloodied husband. "Yes. John was suspicious as soon as they walked in. He said that McFee couldn't have sent them. Then he recognized this —this man, here. Called him Senator Quenton. I guess he's the one you read about in the papers. A very rich man. He hates everybody, but he seems like nothing but a cotton-picker dressed up in Sunday best, to me. They wanted the envelope, but John wouldn't give it to them, and when he insisted on calling McFee again, they wouldn't let him. That man—" She pointed an accusing finger at Hackett. "That man began to do things to John that I never thought —I couldn't believe—" Her mouth shook.

Durell said quickly, "All right, Mrs. Henderson. Go ahead, tie up that man on the porch. Then come back here."

Durell waited until she left. Hackett had made no move to do anything with the water the woman had brought for her husband. Durell wondered at the depth of hatred in him as he looked at Quenton and Hackett. He wanted to use the shotgun then and there. He looked at the tortured man. John Henderson was slumped forward with his slack jaw on his bloody chest. He looked dead. Nothing in heaven or on earth could make the man talk now, Durell thought bitterly. He turned to Quenton, aware of time running out, of pressure along his muscles and nerves.

Quenton said quaveringly, "Durell, we can make a deal, eh? You can join us. I'll give you Hackett's job. I can clear you with the loyalty board. You want that, eh?"

"I don't need or want your fixing," Durell said flatly.

Hackett said thinly, "Like I told you, Senator. He never stole that file. It was given to him, for bait. He's a plant. His job is to get the goods on you."

Quenton's eyes were opaque. "That right? That right, Durell?"

"Right," Durell said. "I started out to tie a can to someone who was pilfering classified data from K Section. We had a line on Gibney, and I worked on it through him. You didn't come into the picture until Hackett dug at me a little, that first night, and made me lose the file. The file was supposed to convince Gibney I was a bona fide traitor."

"I don't believe you," Quenton whispered, shocked.

Hackett laughed. "You goddamn senile fool! Stop dribbling and let Durell lay it on the line. Maybe you can still buy us out."

"No deals," Durell said. "No buys."

"But you can't prove anything," Quenton whispered. He sat in his chair like a shriveled spider, and his head rocked back and forth on his pipestem neck. Durell wondered how he could once have conceived of this little monster as dangerous. Even Hackett exhibited only contempt for him. Durell frowned. He felt for an instant as if he had put a finger on one incongruity more important than anything else he had discovered.

"What are you after, Quenton?" he asked. "What's the purpose of your Q Board? Why all the foaming at the mouth about patriotism and loyalty? Why set up an elaborate blackmail system to get government clerks and brass alike under your dirty thumb?"

"Tell him," Hackett said. He laughed silently. "Maybe Durell will buy it."

"There's too much talk about peace," Quenton whispered.

"Too *much?*" Durell asked.

Quenton seemed hypnotized by Durell's shotgun. His tongue flicked over his lips in the manner of an old man adjusting his dentures. "They'll trick us," he whispered. "It's all lies, see? All smiles and soft talk, while they get ready to throw the bomb at us. Well, we got to drop the bomb first. Never mind what they say at Geneva, never mind those fool conferences! Hit 'em now, while they think they got us fooled and off guard."

Durell felt incredulous. "You don't really believe that's the best thing to do?"

"It's the only thing!" Quenton's voice was stronger, but it assumed the singsong quality of a parrot. "The only way we can be safe is to destroy 'em, once and for all. Wipe 'em off the earth!"

"You're talking about the deaths of millions of people."

"They don't count," Quenton said with contempt. "They ain't hardly human, them slaves over there."

"And the Americans who will die? They'll drop bombs on us, too. The cities will be wiped out, the country laid waste. Suppose we win at that cost? What then?"

Quenton grinned slyly. "Then there won't be so many big Yankee mouths around sayin' how to run things. There'll be fewer to share in what's left. Anyway, it's survival of the fittest, hey, Amos?" He appealed to Hackett. "I ain't so good at explaining. Amos knows the line we're gonna follow when we get the war started. Amos don't worry about gettin' killed himself. We got it all planned. We'll be safe. Our people in Washington know what to do, too, when the bombs come. We'll come out when it's all over and show them snooty labor bastards and city folk what the score is. We'll run things right."

"How many people have you got lined up in key government spots?" Durell asked quietly.

"Hundreds. Thousands."

"All organized?"

"Every department can be reconstructed from scratch, using our own people to head things."

"You must have an extensive filing system," Durell suggested.

Quenton's eyes were suddenly veiled. "Not so extensive. We don't need a big setup to control it." Hatred edged his words. It was the voice of a cropper, illiterate, prejudiced, fanatical with resentment. "I waited a long time for this, Durell. Times were when I never figured a way to get even. I took a lot of dirt when I was a boy, and then I found the oil, and the oil got me cattle, and then some folks liked my ideas and put me into politics. I learned me how to live good. But I ain't never forgot what it's like to be hungry. I'll never be hungry again. We got to think right in this country! We got to do right! We can't ever sit down and talk to them fellers over there. They'll knife us in the back and take everything away from us, everything I ever got. But I won't let 'em. Trouble is," the old man said, his voice dropping, a sly insane wink squeezing one side of his face, "folks don't know what's best for 'em. So we do it this way. Start trouble over there, make 'em mad, make 'em shoot down a couple of our planes. Get folks stirred up so we can throw the bomb, start the war. When it's over, we run things."

Durell watched the loose, wet mouth of the old man work back and forth in his tirade. Quenton went on, but Durell no longer listened. This was not the true face of his enemy, this senile old man who had terrorized the nation's capital, this old man like a bottle filled to the brim with crazy hatreds and crazier plans for dominating those who had kicked him and starved him when he was a boy long ago. There was nothing to fear here. The balance wheel of sanity in the nation could control this old man with his ranting, raving poisons.

The real danger was elsewhere. In another face, still shadowy, still hidden, in another mind that was cool and clever, intelligent enough to hide behind this overt mask of political lunacy.

He looked at Hackett.

The saturnine man was smiling, and as Durell met his dark gaze he caught a flash of comprehension in the conspirator's eyes.

Hackett said, "You're getting the picture now, Durell."

"Is it you?" Durell asked. He was touched by a terrible fear. "You're the one who's fed the old man this nonsense?"

"It's not nonsense. It can happen."

"And they're your ideas?"

"No. Not mine."

"Then there's someone else. Who is it?" Durell asked.

The fear grew in him. It was like a dark spreading wave shot through with chuckling white. He had made a mistake and overlooked the most obvious answer of all. He did not want Hackett. He knew what Hackett was. The answer was not here in this frothing old man, and not in Hackett, the man who carried out orders with violence as his weapon. The enemy was safely hidden behind a dark curtain. He could not see his face. But he would learn to know it.

He stared at Hackett. His finger tightened on the shotgun trigger and Hackett saw this and something changed in his face.

His smile faded. "Wait a moment."

"I want to know his name," Durell said.

"I don't know it! I swear, I'm not lying, I don't know it!"

Mrs. Henderson came back suddenly from the porch, where she had been tying up the guard. She paused in the doorway and the back of her hand went up to her mouth. Her whisper was a lost, forlorn sound.

"John?"

Durell looked at her husband. John Henderson would never tell where he had hidden the file. Death had come into the room in the last few moments.

And Hackett chose that instant to jump for freedom.

chapter TWENTY-ONE

HE SPRANG like a great dark cat for Durell's shotgun, his face stamped with a final desperation that changed, even as he jumped, into total despair. Durell chopped with the barrel of the shotgun and the man dropped as if pole-axed. Durell hit him again. He stood over the prone figure with the shotgun clubbed, shaking, murder in him. He wanted to kill Hackett. He wanted to slash the life out of the man sprawled at his feet. Hackett's face was a mask of blood. Only his dark eyes were alive, still lighted by one final, despairing plea. Blood trickled from his thin mouth.

"Please . . ." Mrs. Henderson whispered.

Her voice cut through the rage in Durell's mind. He stepped back as the woman knelt beside the crumpled body of her husband.

"Please don't kill that man," the woman said.

"He killed your husband."

"One sin does not justify another."

Durell looked for Quenton. The little man was gone.

Instantly he jumped over Hackett's figure, slammed through the door. The hall ran from front to back of the house. The front screen door was just closing. He spun on his toes, lunged that way.

"Quenton!"

He hit the porch, feet thudding on the planks. He still held the shotgun as a club. He reversed it now, searching the dark shadows. The little man had vanished.

"Quenton!"

The moonlight mocked him.

He circled the porch, came around the back, and faced the barn. Deirdre, Art Greenwald, and Tommy Henderson were running across the yard toward him. Art had a gun in his hand. Durell stepped over the guard Mrs. Henderson had tied up and went to meet them. Fear crawled in him. He knew he was going to be too late now.

"Tommy, what did your father do with the file?"

"I don't— What's been going on?" the boy asked.

"You know where he hid it, don't you?"

"Why don't you ask him? If he's willing to tell you—"

"I can't ask him. He's dead. Quick, now! Where is it?"

"In the barn—his machine bench . . ." The boy's voice trailed off as he understood what Durell had said. "Dead?"

Durell turned, ran toward the barn. Art called after him, then thudded heavily in his tracks. There was a light switch just inside the wide doors. A smell of new hay filled the close summer air. Floodlights turned the yard into a dazzling glare, lighted a flight of stairs going up to a loft. A workbench stood under a cobwebbed window under the roof overhang. Durell swung toward it, pulled open tool drawers at random, let the tools clatter and thump to the dusty plank floor.

He found the envelope in the third drawer.

Ten minutes later they were in Greenwald's car. Headlights hit them, spraying the road and bushes on either hand. The banshee wail of a police siren spiraled up to a crescendo as the patrol car rocketed past them. They were almost at the Potomac bridges to Washington. Deirdre sat on the front seat between Durell and Art Greenwald.

The patrol car slammed past without slackening speed.

"Who called *them?*" Art muttered.

"Quenton. He needs time. And we need time, too."

"What have you got in mind, Sam? Why not grab Quenton? He couldn't have been far away from that farm."

"Quenton isn't important. He's only the front man, the tool of the man we want," Durell said.

"And who is that, for God's sake?"

"I don't know yet."

"Somebody at Number Twenty Annapolis?"

"Right."

He felt Deirdre shivering, although the night was warm. She hadn't spoken much. Her hand rested on his arm, and from the tail of his eye he saw her finely chiseled profile, pale and taut against the flickering swords of light that slipped in and out of the car. He looked at his watch. "What time did you say the guard changes at Number Twenty?"

"Midnight," Greenwald said.

It was eleven-forty-seven.

Deirdre stood on the corner with him. The street was hot, dark, silent. The trees were motionless in their neat little squares cut out of the concrete pavement. A single window was lighted on the third floor of Number Twenty Annapolis Street. McFee's window. Art had been gone for more than five minutes. He was due back now.

Deirdre said, "Sam, how can you be sure?"

"There is no other answer."

"But—McFee?"

"I didn't say it was McFee."

"But what can you find that will prove it?"

"Names. Items for blackmail. The Q files."

"In McFee's office?"

He looked at her. She looked beautiful. He wondered how he could have conceived of life without her. He regretted everything he had been forced to do to hurt her. He wished it were all over, and then he wished none of it had started, and then he looked down the street for Art and there was nobody at all.

"Where in hell is Art?"

"Sam, I don't understand. What about Quenton?"

"Not important now."

"Or Hackett?"

"He's nobody."

"And that girl, Corinne?"

"It could be Sidonie."

"*Sidonie?*"

"Does that shock you?"

"I can't believe it."

He did not reply. Art was coming down the street, walking with what seemed a casual gait, but actually moving very fast. Durell went to meet him. Art's dark round head bobbed in a quick nod. His mouth was tight, disapproving.

"This is crazy. If Quenton thinks you're heading this way, why won't he tip off Security?"

"He won't," Durell said. "He'll only tip off the man who feeds him all that crazy pap that's stuffed in his senile head."

"It might be too late," Art muttered.

"Damn it, can we get in or can't we?"

"I don't like this."

"To hell with what you like or don't like. Can we get in?"

"Kelly was on guard," Art said. "I told him he was wanted over at D Department."

"And he went?"

"Kelly trusts me," Art said bitterly.

Their feet whispered on the tiled corridor floor. Somewhere a teletype clattered, a bell pinged. Some of the rear offices were lighted, doors shut, as the night crew kept watch over an uneasy peace. Durell drifted like a shadow ahead of Deirdre and Greenwald. The glass panel in McFee's door shimmered blankly. He tried the knob. Not locked. He looked at Art. Greenwald stood like a dark, sullen bear. They spoke in whispers.

"I want to go in here alone," Durell said.

"What are you going to do?" Art asked.

"Search the files. Turn 'em upside down."

"Are you crazy? They'll know."

"Everybody's got to know, anyway." Durell looked at Deirdre. "I'm starting with Sidonie's office. It might be wired. If I tap off an alarm, I don't want either of you caught with me. No use our all going under if the thing falls wrong."

Greenwald was sweating. "Sam, it's a wild gamble. You've got your file back. You can clear things with McFee now."

"Suppose McFee is the man I want?"

"I don't believe that."

"But suppose he is?" Durell insisted.

Greenwald stood, shaking his head. Durell opened the door. "Go, both of you. Wait for me outside."

He went in and closed the door against them, leaned back against it, listened to their footsteps hesitate, then move away. It was hot and still in the office. Faint light seeped through the glass panel behind him, touched Sidonie's desk, the charts on the wall, the door to McFee's inner office, the filing cabinets. Where to begin? What he wanted must be found here, or never found at all. He had no illusions about the safety that the recovery of the lost envelope might lend him. Too much had happened, too many people were involved.

He began his search. He knew how to ransack a room quickly and neatly, without waste motion, without loss of time over nonessentials. Yet the job might consume several hours. How much time did he have? He did not know. Time was a dead weight leaning on him, threatening to crush him at any moment. He lit a cigarette, looked beyond Sidonie's desk into the Spartan simplicity of McFee's office.

McFee, he thought. Who knew anything about the General, who kept tabs on *him*? Gibney had received a call from McFee about his son's death—and Burritt Swayney showed up at the island. The farmer Henderson had phoned McFee—and Quenton and Hackett showed up at the farm. Who was the spy, and who was the loyal man? He lit a cigarette, dragged deeply, and walked into McFee's office to search there.

Or maybe it was Sidonie. Her husband's death had been a

cruel blow, months ago, enough to embitter her against a cause that brought such personal devastation. Who had reached her, and why?

Suddenly Durell halted his search. There was a shadow in the back of his mind, using personal secrets as a lever to further Quenton's ends. He let the shadow grow, straining for a more definite outline. A dim flame of excitement flickered in him. He stood very still. He stared at the three telephones on McFee's desk, and wished now that Art Greenwald were still with him. But he knew enough about Art's work to make a quick survey. Moving suddenly, he found a small pocket tool in McFee's desk and took one of the telephones apart, found nothing in it, went to work on the second. The building was silent except for the distant pinging of a teletype machine. He wondered where Art and Deirdre were waiting. Not too far away. These long moments would be hard on Deirdre, not knowing, unable to guess what the next minute might bring.

The second telephone was normal, too.

And the third.

He sat down in McFee's chair, hands flat on the desk, staring at nothing at all. An electric clock on the desk read twelve-twenty. He watched the sweep hand circle, heard the muted whir of the motor. He stiffened. Quickly he picked up the clock, studied its face, considered the back plate. The wire seemed thicker than the tiny motor called for. The tool in his hand gave him quick access to the screws that held the plate in place. It clattered to the desk and he pulled the goose-neck lamp closer to study the interior mechanism.

The outer office door opened and closed quietly.

Burritt Swayney, chief of K Section, stood in the entrance.

"Keep your hands right where they are, Sam."

Durell looked past the glare of the lamp. "Hello, Burritt."

"I kept listening to you get warmer for the last ten minutes. I guess it was too much to hope that you might give it up. You're too damned stubborn for that."

"You bugged McFee's office with this mike in his clock?"

"My job," Swayney said, nodding.

"The hell."

"Think what you like. Keep your hands right there, Sam. I wouldn't mind killing you here and now. I'd get a medal, hey?" Swayney heeled the door shut behind him. "Anyone with you?"

"You heard it all. I'm alone."

"Anybody in the building with you?"

"Not that I know of."

"Deirdre?"

"No."

"Don't lie, Sam."

"To hell with you," Durell said.

Burritt Swayney, he thought. The human memory machine. The walking filing cabinet. Defeat loomed black in his mind. How do you pry facts from a man's brain? How do you present memorized data as evidence to an investigating board? It couldn't be done. No federal grand jury would touch it.

Swayney smiled, standing short and fat, his neat gray suit and bow tie as prim as ever. His mouth pursed, sucked air. He held a small .32 revolver pointed at Durell. He chuckled.

"End of the road, hey? I never discounted you, Sam, but you moved faster than I thought."

"You knew about my assignment?"

"Of course. I know all of McFee's deals."

"So you were ready for me. You knew I was meeting Colonel Gibney at the Triton Country Club two nights ago. That's why you sent Hackett and two of the Q men after me."

"Have you got that file?" Swayney asked.

"Yes, I have it."

"Hand it over, then."

"You'll have to take it off my dead body," Durell said.

"That will be a pleasure, Sam. You'd like it here?" Swayney asked in his soft, prissy voice. "You want to die right now?"

Durell just stared at him.

Swayney looked puzzled. "Who knows you're here, Sam?"

Durell laughed. "You're finished, Burritt. Blow your brains out. Slit your throat. Go back to that dried-up prune of a wife you've got and weep on her shoulder. Don't count on Quenton. You've got the old man tied up like a pretzel. He tipped you, didn't he? He told you I got the file back. McFee will believe me now. He'll back me."

"Shut up," Swayney whispered. His round face shook, and little muscles jumped and jerked and made the soft flesh quiver. "Give me that file."

"You can't use it now, Burritt. The game is over."

"How did you circle around and come back to me, Sam?"

"It was easy," Durell said. "We had a traitor in K Section." You look here and there, you take up with this one and that. Somebody had to fit the picture. And you fit it, Burritt. Perfectly. McFee called Colonel Gibney about the death of his son, and you promptly showed up on the island. Your big mistake. You gained nothing by it, lost everything. I suppose you had to do something about Mary Gibney. Did you panic, Burritt? Is that why you killed her?"

"You think I killed her?"

"I'm sure you did. She was going to tell me about you. And you knew that once she knew her son was dead, she had nothing to fear from you. You couldn't hurt her any more; you no longer had a hold over her. Did you keep her in line, with Colonel Gibney, by implying that Roger would be killed over there if she didn't go along? Your mistake, Burritt. You contacted her personally, instead of letting Hackett do that particular job. She couldn't stomach Hackett, so you took over in this one instance. So she knew you for what you are. And you hurried to the island to shut her mouth by strangling her."

"Go ahead, keep talking. I want to know what you know."

Durell said easily, "There's no harm in digging the hole deeper for you. You tapped McFee's office by putting a bug in the clock here. You did it yourself, because you couldn't trust Art Greenwald to do it for you. You used Corinne to get accessory information. You with your calculator of a mind. Nothing slips by you, nothing is forgotten. You're the spy we wanted, Burritt. You're the traitor that McFee sent me to get. You fit the shadow pattern. You showed up when only McFee or someone with a pipeline into McFee's office could know enough to show up."

"Go on, hey?"

"Tell me about Quenton," Durell said. "What's his background?"

"He's an old fool," Swayney said.

"Tell me about him."

There was a weakness in Swayney, a point of vanity, and Durell had touched it lightly and tentatively. It worked. Swayney's face changed, took on a faint asperity, the face of superiority, as he called on his phenomenal memory.

"Share-cropper, born 1881 in Jennifer, Texas," Swayney said. "Poor parents, hand-to-mouth existence, no formal education beyond the third grade in grammar school. Worked for an old man named Jason Nyland, was given some apparently worthless speculative land holdings when Nyland died in 1916. Ran a wildcat rig on the land, hit a gusher, landed on top of the heap with millions you can't count. Went hog-wild—wine, women, song. Some crazy stories about how he carried on. Mixed up in all sorts of lunatic-fringe fronts from the start. For a capitalist, he goes over the edge in hating the common man. Was analyzed after a complete nervous collapse in 1948. I got the analyst's report. Weird stuff. No education, only a swamp of a mind, concerned with keeping what he's got to the point of paranoia. Terrified by the nightmare of being a share-cropper again."

"When did you meet him?" Durell asked easily.

"In the Senate. I was called before his committee," Swayney replied. "He liked me. We, ah—had interests in common."

"Women?"

"He likes women."

"He's an old man," Durell objected.

"So was King David when he had girls warm his bed and bones for him."

"You arranged a happy night life for him?"

"We got along."

"And you fed him the idea of securing safety for his wealth only by getting to run things himself."

Swayney smiled. "That is correct."

"So you might be called the mastermind behind Quenton's wild ravings. You tell him what to say and do. But you organize, you really control the whole Q outfit."

"Right."

"With the ultimate aim of controlling the government."

"Right."

"By means of blackmail, spotting key people in key departments?"

"Right, right."

"But the new talks about peace upset you, Burritt, is that it?"

"In a war, society is uprooted," Swayney said. He smiled, holding his gun easily, looked at Durell with hatred. "A cold war isn't enough. Since Geneva and the conferences afterward, it looks as if there may not be a war, after all. That would be too bad. It's the only way I can get where I want to go. To the top, hey? Not impossible. You say I'm only a small bureaucrat, that my ambition is insanely grand? So was Napoleon, and he was a common soldier; so was Hitler, and he was even less. In times of stress, anyone from any level may rise, if he's prepared for it, if he's ready to take destiny in both hands and make use of chaos for his own ends."

"You don't count the millions of lives lost, the homes destroyed, the cities and nations laid waste?"

"Don't lecture me on your puerile moralities, Sam."

"And can you trust your people after this holocaust? Can you trust those you force into stealing our confidential items and shooting them across the sea to create tensions with the aim of inducing somebody, somewhere, to order a bomb dropped?"

"I have them all on file."

"In your head?"

"Right, right."

"You're lying," Durell said. "You can't remember that much."

Swayney looked angry. "Lying?"

"There has to be concrete evidence. Photographs, pornography, perhaps, illicit affairs by which your people have been trapped into working for Q. You have photostats, affidavits, tucked away somewhere."

"Naturally."

"Where, Burritt?"

Swayney did not reply. He seemed to be listening to something beyond the closed office door. Durell listened, too. He did not hear anything. He kept his eye on Swayney's gun. He did not underestimate Swayney. He knew that he had not disarmed the man with the talk he had evoked from him. Swayney would kill him. He had to. He felt the doors closing, one by one, all around him. There was no way out. Not once had the gun wavered from its point-blank aim, and if the shot was triggered, Swayney would become a hero.

And somewhere in Europe another man would squeeze off a shot, and a high official would fall to an assassin's bullet. Out of the ensuing charges of treachery, deceit, and plot would evolve an equation that spelled atomic war.

Durell moved his hands slightly on the desk.

"Don't," Swayney said. "Where is the file you recovered?"

"Here," Durell told him. "In my pocket."

"Which pocket?"

"Inside, left."

"Are you armed?"

"Yes."

"Don't move, Sam. Just don't move."

Swayney left his position by the door and came around the desk. He put the gun to Durell's head. The muzzle grated painfully against his scalp, just above his ear. He smelled the oil on the barrel, and the shave lotion that Swayney used, and the heat in the summer fabric of Swayney's suit. It was all over. Only seconds were left. He had no doubt that Swayney would fire the moment he was sure he had the papers he wanted.

"What will you do with the file?" Durell asked.

His voice sounded strange in the silent office.

"Send it over there," Swayney said. "Let them know that Antonio works for us. Let them think we're on a program of assassination. They're as frightened of us as we are wary of them. There's no trust or faith in them. Maybe they will welcome the excuse to try to bomb us."

"They won't just try. They will."

"All right, so they will, hey?"

"And suppose you're killed by one of the bombs, Burritt?"

"It's not likely to happen."

"There's no place you can hide from it. Don't you know that?"

Swayney said, "You're making me nervous, Sam. Keep your hands as they are. Don't move a hair." With a quick gesture, Swayney flipped open Durell's coat, removed the gun Art Greenwald had given him, dropped it in the wastebasket, and took the Manila envelope as well. "It's been opened," Swayney said. "Have you checked inside?"

"I haven't had time. But it's probably what you want."

Swayney put it in his pocket and retreated a step. "Are you afraid now, Sam?"

"Yes, I'm afraid. For the whole world." Durell turned his head and looked at the small, fat man. He saw in Swayney's face all the prejudice, all the narrow bigotry and fanatical ambition he had always fought against. Maybe Swayney would win the last battle, after all. Maybe this is the way the world ends, he thought—in the fat little hands of Burritt Swayney. He said, "Will you kill me here?"

"Why not?"

"It will raise some questions—why I came back, what I'm doing in Dickinson McFee's office, at his desk, at this time of night. Why I risked capture to get in here, and how I managed to enter the building at all."

Swayney's mouth dropped open. "What did you say?"

"Think about it, Burritt."

"How *did* you get in here?"

"It was easy."

"You had an accomplice? Someone helped you get the guard out of the way!" Swayney's voice lifted. "Who was it, Sam?"

Durell shook his head. "You see how it is, Burritt? You won't be made safe simply by shooting me. You'll have to go on shooting."

"Was it Deirdre?"

"She has no authority to order the guard away."

Swayney was sweating. "McFee? You got to him, convinced him you hadn't crossed him on your assignment?"

"You'll have to find that out yourself."

"Answer me!" Swayney shouted.

Durell laughed at him.

And Swayney swung the gun in a raking blow across Durell's face.

Durell was waiting, hoping, ready.

His arm came up, blocked the blow, caught the gun, and drove it down. It went off with a violent crash. Wood splinters flew and a scar appeared on McFee's desk. Swayney made a squalling sound, a noise compounded of pain, anguish, and frustration. His pale eyes were incredulous as Durell came up out of the chair. Durell hit him, felt the crunch of breaking cartilage, hit him again. The gun fell to the floor. Swayney dodged back, squirmed, twisted, ran for the door. Durell lunged after him. Swayney yanked open the door, yelling for help. His voice echoed hysterically through the dark corridors of the building.

Art Greenwald appeared at the end of the hall. Swayney ran toward him, screaming for Art to shoot Durell. Greenwald looked past him to Durell's tall figure in the doorway. Durell nodded. Greenwald caught Swayney's fat, flying form and bounced him off the wall.

Swayney's mouth hung open. Saliva dripped and drooled from his loose lips.

Greenwald hit him once, hard, with finality. Swayney's mouth closed and his eyes closed and he went down to the floor.

chapter TWENTY-TWO

DICKINSON McFee walked restlessly up and down, his normally tidy military figure in dishevelment. He said, "Damn it all, why didn't you come to me straight off? Why chase all over the countryside? If I hadn't dropped into Greenwald's place an hour ago, I'd never have stumbled on Corinne there and got the story from her. Chances are, I'd still be in the dark. Why not come to me, Sam?"

A doctor was puttering with a cut on Durell's face. His antiseptic swab stung and burned.

"Would you have believed me, General?" Durell asked quietly.

McFee halted as if struck. "Damn it, no."

"All right, then."

"But you took one hell of a chance!"

"It was a gamble, but it had to work." Durell shrugged. "Somebody was tapping your phone conversations with a bug in that electric clock. It was either Sidonie or Swayney. Have you found the recorder in Swayney's office?"

"Yes, we found it."

"And the documentary addenda to Swayney's memory files?"

"Tucked away under Q, in his personal office records. Of all the goddamn, brazen nerve!"

McFee's office was crowded. A teletype kept rattling in Sidonie's office beyond the doorway, and men came and went irregularly. State was in a flap. The FBI was in consultation. The White House wanted to be kept informed. Durell sat back in his chair and let the doctor work on his face. He felt an exhaustion that weighed down every nerve and bone and muscle. He wanted to sleep. But he couldn't sleep.

"Where is Swayney now?"

"In custody. He'll be held for the grand jury. Can't be helped. The publicity will be hell."

"And what about our friend Antonio, over in Budapest?"

McFee made a quick, hard grimace. "Shot and killed four hours ago while attempting to knock off the visiting dignitary from Moscow. There's much emotional howling over there, but nothing to connect us with it. Antonio died instantly. No sweat now. A good man, but unstable. There won't be any kickback."

"I'm sorry for him," Durell said. "And Quenton?"

"In a hospital. Complete collapse, physically and mentally. Nothing there, either. His organization is done for. We've got Hackett salted away. There isn't anybody else important." McFee pushed aside the fussy doctor and stood in front of Durell, hand thrust out. "Welcome back, Sam."

"You little son-of-a-bitch," Durell said. He pushed back his chair, stood up, and reached for his coat.

McFee said, "Wait a minute."

"You put me through a grinder and then just say welcome back?"

"What would you have me do?"

"You could have believed me, you could have trusted me."

"No. I couldn't."

"All right, then. Go to hell."

He walked out, clad in bitterness.

Nobody stopped him. McFee made a quick sign, and stared after him as his men made way for Durell, and Durell left the building walking alone.

It was almost dawn, in that brief moment between starlight and the first delicate streak of gray in the east. The air was cool, the street glistened with dew that dripped from the sycamore trees. There was no traffic. His heels made hollow echoes on the wet brick sidewalk.

He drew a deep breath, and another. There would be peace. Men were still wrapped in the shackles of war, still chained and trapped by suspicion and inherited hate and diverse fears. It could not be shaken off all at once. But one day, certainly not tomorrow or next month or next year, his job would become obsolete, as useless as that of a feudal squire assisting his liege lord with armor, gauntlets, and spear. Yet by his continued existence for today, the peace might gradually and painfully be secured. Accidents would happen. A man deranged by grief over the loss of his love, thousands of miles from this street and this city, could still trigger old hatreds and primitive fears in the beast who might manipulate the intricate electronics of an atomic bomb. A senile old man in terror for his hoard could be deluded into the belief that slaughter and destruction were all for the best. A frustrated man of brilliant intellect could induce the old man to act for him in a dream to gain power.

Swayney's nightmare had been no more impossible of achievement than the dreams of a recent paperhanger or the ambitions of a Corsican artillerist, true. Swayney had not been alone in imagining himself to be unique, starred by destiny.

But it was over, and he felt only a negative emptiness, and no sense of achievement.

Because it would happen again.

There would be other dangers, in other times.

Durell came to a halt.

A car was parked at the corner, and when he stopped on the sidewalk the door flew open and Deirdre came running toward him, crying his name.

"Sam? What is it? Are you all right?"

He looked at her. "It's all over."

"But what's wrong? Where are you going?"

"I just resigned," he told her.

The street light looked dim and feeble now in the gray light of the new dawn. A cool breeze stirred the leaves of the sycamore trees, and they rustled and rattled over his head. The girl's eyes searched his face.

"You're angry because you were alone, because McFee didn't believe you or trust you?"

"Yes, I'm angry," Durell said.

"But what would you have done in McFee's place?"

He saw her beauty and her goodness and all the anxiety of her love for him.

"McFee trusted me. He should have trusted me all the way."

"But he couldn't," she argued. "And you couldn't ever leave your job, Sam. It's part of you. And you didn't answer my question: Given McFee's job, would you have acted any differently?"

He thought about it. He tried to imagine what he would do if his resignation went into effect. He saw a dreary wasteland ahead of him, a uselessness, a spectator's life. His anger ebbed. He laughed at himself, at the moment's pique, the anger he had felt.

"Let's go back, Sam," Deirdre said.

"Not yet."

"But you—"

"There's plenty of time," he said. "I'll see McFee later. I'm sure he'll be waiting."

He took her arm and her fingers quickly locked in his and he turned her away. They walked together, with no questions asked as to their destination.